THE ARTIST'S DREAM

Stories and Pictures by
IAN BREAKWELL

SERPENT'S
TAIL

Why so much fear of tears? Because the masks we use are made of salt. A stinging, red salt which makes us beautiful and majestic but devours our skin.

Luisa Valenzuela

Other titles in the **MASKS** series

Michael Bracewell	**The Crypto-Amnesia Club**
Leslie Dick	**Without Falling**
Juan Goytisolo	**Landscapes After the Battle**
Luisa Valenzuela	**The Lizard's Tail**

British Library Cataloguing in Publication Data

Breakwell, Ian
The artist's dream.
I. Title
823'.914[F]   PR6052.R3/

ISBN 1-85242-114-2

First published 1988 by
Serpent's Tail Ltd
27 Montpelier Grove
London NW5

Layout and design by Fiona Keating
Phototypeset by AKM Associates (UK) Ltd

Printed in Great Britain by
Commercial Colour Press, London

CONTENTS

ACKNOWLEDGEMENTS

Some of these texts first appeared in the following publications: *Summit*, Gallery Ten, London 1967; *Calendar*, Transformaction, Devon 1971; *Fiction Texts*, Third Eye Centre, Glasgow 1978; *Monologues and Dialogues*, Carlisle Museum, Carlisle 1981; *Rural Tales*, Galloping Dog Press, Newcastle upon Tyne 1986; and in the magazines Artscribe, Circa, and The Looker.

Ian Breakwell's paintings, drawings and collages reproduced by courtesy of the artist; Anthony Reynolds Gallery, London; Galeria Fernando Vijande, Madrid; Arts Council of Great Britain; Eastern Arts Association.

The publishers would like to thank the following for the use of photographs of original artwork: Robin Klassnik, Matts Gallery (frontispiece, endpiece); Norman Stafford, Tyne Tees Television (pages 90, 92); Karen Knorr (46); Susan Ormerod (82, 83); John Hall (86, 87); Jack Cutter, Tyne Tees Television (48, 104, 105); Francis Murgatroyd (27, 32, 33, 94); Audio Visual Centre, University of East Anglia (38, 40, 42); all other photographs by Ian Breakwell.

ILLUSTRATIONS

THE SUMMIT

T he summit can only be the "top". This particular summit is a flat plateau surmounting a pyramidal mound which is composed of an anonymous material, grey-brown in colour. The mound is situated in a white void, and so it is difficult to estimate its size, or the size of the plateau. Standing on the plateau are six approximately oblong organisms; they are definitely not inanimate objects, because even in the still atmosphere on the plateau they each quiver slightly at intermittent intervals. This quivering is initially confusing to an onlooker, because when one or more of the oblongs quiver and the others stay motionless, the onlooker might be led to think that there are individual differences between the organisms: for instance, that on this plateau there are at least two kinds of organisms: those that quiver and those that do not; whereas if he were to continue his observation he would be certain to see all the oblong organisms quiver in turn in an identical manner; also, if he kept watch on the plateau for a long enough time he would see all six quiver simultaneously. He would instantly realise that his original mental division of the organisms was mistaken. However, as the rotation of quivering activity appeared to have no set pattern, then it is obvious that the onlooker might have to watch for a considerable time before he saw all the possible permutations of activity; before he realised that the oblongs were identical not only in activity but also in colouring and size; that each organism was identically covered on all sides with vertical black stripes, almost like veins; that each organism was semi-transparent; that what he had believed to be differences in size, form and colouring had merely been optical illusions caused by the rapid quivering; but he would see these things only if they became apparent during his period of observation, and who could blame him for turning away, satisfied with his observations, unaware that they were incorrect? Who can say how long he would have had to keep watch before he saw the real state of affairs on the summit? He was no professional observer, under no obligation to report comprehensively on all visible details; he was merely a passer-by who, finding himself one day with a clear view of the summit, stopped and gazed at the colony on the plateau, before continuing on his way. At the time he did not consider that there was anything unusual about what he had seen; although he personally never had a clear view of the plateau before, he assumed that others had done so, in fact for all he knew it was an everyday occurrence. It was only later, when in conversation with friends he mentioned his clear view of the plateau, that it became apparent by their surprise — they were not astonished, merely surprised — that far from being an everyday occurrence, on the contrary, to see what he had seen was rare. The more he and his friends mentioned his experience to other people, the more it was suggested that perhaps he was the only person ever to have had such a clear view of the summit; in fact no one could remember any person seeing the plateau even indistinctly. Of course everyone assumed its existence: every mound or mountain must have a summit; it was merely that not one person could ever recollect having seen it. A subtle change now occurred in this chance observer's attitude to what he had seen. At first he had attached little importance to his experience, until his attention was focused on it by the surprised reactions of his friends; he was now forced to think again about something he might otherwise have forgotten. He tried to be objective; admittedly he had viewed the plateau in a casual manner, at the time he had seen no reason to do otherwise, nevertheless, in retrospect he felt that he could describe his view with reasonable accuracy; he had always been proud of his good memory, and he vowed that he would only give an account of that which he could clearly remember; this he tried to do whenever people asked him to describe what he had seen, as many now did. For a time he became something of a local celebrity, although he was shrewd enough not to accept every drink offered to him as encouragement to his description, realising how easy it would be for him to become one more bar-room bore, button-holing visitors to the village and recounting at length what he had seen on that day long ago; they might even seek him out: a tourist attraction! Not that there seemed to be any possibility of international or even national interest in the incident; even the local newspapers had made only half-hearted attempts to follow up the rumours they were certain to hear in such a small community. This did not worry him unduly; he had attached such little importance to the event at first that this, he was sure, had conditioned his attitude to any growth of interest by other people. He had too much to do everyday to be interrupted by the endless questions of reporters, many of them no doubt speaking annoyingly little of his native tongue, perhaps none at all, which would mean the added inconvenience of an interpreter; and they wanting only to know about this episode which had occupied such a tiny fraction of his time. If he tried to tell them of his day-to-day business, of the intricacies of his particular type of buying and selling, which, although he was willing to admit he might be biased, he nevertheless found fascinating, would they be interested? Of course not!

THE PREPARATIONS FOR THE FESTIVAL

Entertainment to suit all tastes.

A first-class buffet for the three hundred dancers.

Children plan to win trophies by riding all types of animals.

Temporary cleaners are hired for the carpet emporium.

Reporters have more news than they can handle.

The extra two thousand disposable milk containers to be used during the week would so burden available removal facilities that substantial local authority investment had to be undertaken immediately.

Who will plan the seating arrangements? A committee is formed: there are representatives from the town council, the cultural committee, the fire brigade, local schools, amateur dramatic societies and music clubs.

Food technologists advise where to eat . . . leaflet distributors fan out through the streets . . . soldiers tour schools.

One restaurant advertises a television dancing team.

For the more adventurous there are table-mats depicting a car and cycle in collision.

The Electrical Department deals with the fairy-lights.

By popular demand there is to be a mass display of springboard diving, under the direction of a former resident of the town, who has since become well known in the aquatic athletics world , and has competed in many water-sports events on the West Coast of America.

The canal is sealed for safety, and old slate roofs are waterproofed.

Homes are cleared at short notice . . . shops increase their stocks of camping equipment . . . the Farmers' Association donates three acres of grassland . . . fur cushions are at a premium.

There is a sub-committee to take care of star performers.

An agent confirms that he can arrange for two coach-loads of blind people who end their performance by inviting twelve members of the audience to play miniature xylophones.

Angling associations stake out the river banks, and uproot all weed which shows above the surface of the water.

Historians besiege the library for textbooks.

A manager is in charge of jigsaw puzzles and has autonomous command.

The colour themes of the food were shelved; no-one could agree. Mayonnaise in tubes was the only item on which voting was unanimous.

Miniature television sets are fitted on motor-cycles . . . loudspeakers and leaflets in the streets of the suburbs . . . aircraft also broadcast appeals . . . while at 23.00 hours, with military punctuality, the paratroopers make their distribution of chocolate to the poor people of the parish.

A feeding-table is placed out of doors. While the children are sucking their fill they are marked with paint spots so that they can be easily recognized again in the capacity crowds.

Gangways to the drinks table are roped off for those who will have to travel a long distance. Entry is supervised by a commissionaire.

Housewives volunteer to sweep away cobwebs . . . all applicants at the employment bureau are hired without question, so that property repairs might be completed without delay . . . tours and excursions are arranged . . . chimneys are removed so as not to obscure the sky.

One hundred and eighty carefully chosen voluntary inspectors are situated around the district, and of course never disclose themselves.

Miniature golf is one way of enjoying yourself. Competitions, and the chance to win a prize are also popular.

Uniformed triplets learn to do clever tricks and thus earn rewards.

Rehearsals begin.

CALENDAR

April 8th   He sat waiting at home for three quarters of an hour with his coat on. He was impatient to be taken to finish his work. He decided that he could not wait any longer. He walked the three miles to the department. Walking in the main entrance he almost collided with a man and a woman carrying equipment. He handed his coat to the girl at the desk. He walked through to the courtyard where his older relatives shuffled with walking-aids and glided in wheelchairs. He took several photographs of his grandfather and his uncle; his uncle repeatedly held up a large doll behind his grandfather's head. He spoke for ten minutes with his aunt, who still bore the scars which had thrilled the crowds. His cousin lay against a pillar trying to join two plastic bricks; her father lay beside her with his hand between her legs. His mother and father were playing cards, although his father would have preferred billiards. Another aunt was emptying ashtrays, while at a grand piano a professional musician played a waltz. Other members of the family combined their efforts. At 10 a.m. a man arrived with a money collecting machine and they each gave the man ninepence; the machine was then used to detect the amount of money involved. Again he talked with his grandfather and touched the stubble on his soft skin. He walked indoors; from the wallbars on one side of the gymnasium hung all his uncles except one. On the other side of the room ball games were being played.

April 9th   He is covered with flags.

April 10th   She thrust the two children over the counter and left the office. Off she went with her seeing-eye dog, Duchess, to Switzerland and

learned to ski; she won a slalom race just following the sound of her instructor as she whizzed between the flags. After that she learned rebound tumbling on the trampolines; came third in the downhill tightrope race.

April 11th　From behind the screen he imitated the voices of three butchers engaged in a conversation which was interrupted by the barking of a dog.

April 12th–19th　He worked an eight-hour day polishing chessmen.

April 19th–22nd　He appeared constantly in public.

April 23rd　The sound of large dice being slowly turned over and over through the corridors of the junior school . . . The hollow murmur of a multitude of skaters.

April 24th　He walks across the road at the traffic lights. In the bar on the corner groups of young people are giving demonstrations of whistling. There appears to be some kind of competition. But even they sit down when she stands up; she is well known in the town, having made several appearances on television. She stands by the side of a rustic bench against a painted backdrop of trees and parkland. Her clothes are simple: a black straw hat, black coat, dress, stockings and shoes; they draw attention to her smiling face. She stands with her hands folded, holding a cream suede purse. At an early age, when her ability was already widely acknowledged, she had agreed to the removal of her tongue, and to its being replaced by a segment of cling peach, which fitted into a slot in the base of her mouth. Although the slice of peach deteriorated rapidly, and in fact had to be replaced daily and before each performance, it did nevertheless result in a melodic warbling whistle which was unique and always greatly admired. Her performance on this evening was of her usual high standard. She was warmly applauded.

He walks into the ballroom and orders a drink. He stands at the extreme end of the bar, on the left. At the opposite end of the bar stands a man in a blue suit. The man in the blue suit moves slowly to his left with his hands on the bar rail, until he leans against a woman who also moves to her left. He watches without turning his head, his shoulder braced against the wall, as the line of people, still looking at their drinks, begin to lean on him. He steps quickly aside and reaches for his coat. Someone laughs and offers to buy him a drink, but he says "No."

He walks out into the street and enters the restaurant on the other side. He sits at a table beside a girl in school uniform who is being fed by her mother and father; they break up the food on her plate and push it very gently into her mouth, waiting while she digests it before giving her any more; the girl runs her fingernails down the wall behind her.

He walks past the flickering neon sign into the building. Light orchestral music soaks through the walls. A woman in ski-pants sits at a polished table, licking envelopes.

Everyone has a glass of wine . . . scores of people pour in through one door as others leave by the exit . . . the man in the evening suit stands in the corridor and says "Goodnight" one hundred and twenty-nine times. The restaurant is nearly empty . . . the waitresses fill the sugar bowls.

Then people crowd in, eating potato crisps, forcing their fingers into their mouths and scratching their upper arms. The blue velvet curtains part, and into the spotlight walks the sallow, dwarflike figure of a hydrocephalic boy, naked except for a notice sellotaped to his chest saying: "PRESS MY HEAD AND I WILL SQUEAK". His eyelids droop as he gazes blankly at the surrounding faces. His blotchy penis begins to rise until he stands with a small, hard erection. The patrons throw serviette rings with surprising accuracy onto his penis, shouting "Hoop-la" and smacking their palms on the tables.

April 25th   When he met her he had no coat. He talked to her in the bar, while he played three sentimental records on the juke-box. She pulled food out of her handbag with blind hands. Courageous as a Red Indian, he stared pitilessly at the dachshund which was digging its claws into the damask covering of the couch. At last he returned, his moustache glued to his face.

April 26th   The dull steaming heat of all his railway journeys . . . the carriages are full of thin schoolgirls, walking continually to the Buffet Car and back . . . they can't keep still . . . young mothers with their legs in irons pull their children through the swaying restaurant . . . empty drinks cans roll from one end of the carriage to the other . . . the bang of the carriage door shook her face . . . pigs jumped away from the train.

April 27th   He saves fragments of conversation.

April 28th   He saves split hairs in his mouth.

April 29th   She spent the night picking her fingers and eating small dishes of crisp radishes.

April 30th   When she threw his books onto the floor he tried to hit her. When he moved to hit her she threw six cut-glass tumblers and four toy cars out of the window. He thought: "This bitch shows passion but lacks a sense of property."

May 2nd   She was drunk and he pretended to be. She carried him home; it took three hours. His cruelty was softened by jokes. He pushed up her skirt on the rug in front of the convector fire. The alcohol made him depressed. He was hit with a hundred menus.

His head upright and his mouth open. The laces of his shoes were uncovered. The tips of the long black hairs are white. Each hair is delicately hinged. The raised spots along the back are red. She dances round and round. He ejects a large blob of fluid and then sucks it in again. "Set an example!" someone shouted. The dog on the roof walked round in circles. Small lumps of earth crumble in his fingers.

May 3rd   She figures as a leader in exercises on the horizontal and parallel bars and on the rings.

May 4th   She had been photographed kneeling on the stomachs of a large number of children and young adults.

May 5th   He saw a car parked in the middle of a street. He saw a lorry mount the pavement in order to pass it, while another car had to reverse because it could not get through . . . Water spurted high into the air and onto the road . . . Lorries, heavily loaded with boxes of fruit, drove slowly through the fog.

May 7th   From the telephone kiosk he watches the activity in the centre of the town . . . a slow downhill procession . . . All sound is cut off by the plate-glass. Cars, motor-bikes, lorries and buses cross effortlessly at the junction. The lights change. People hurry across carrying mail. A slow congestion builds up, then the lights change again, and the traffic wheels round past the hoardings. Everything is in bond, even the streets.

May 8th   Sheep encircle the swimming pool.

May 9th   The wall is breached and the stones spill onto the streets. The

pigeon coos softly in the avenue of trees, and the cat lies purring on the parked car. On every corner people are talking about food.

May 10th   Two men face each other behind a wall and grasp their left wrists with their right hands and each other's right wrist with their left hands. The two men stoop down.

May 11th   He collected his money and left . . . his head was a Spanish onion being peeled . . . old women walk towards him on the street.

May 12th   Two-way traffic interlocked at the roundabout.

May 13th   The room was filling with an unusually large number of children. He tunnelled deep into the wall and made a bed. His back reinforced with an artificial hump and his left foot six inches off the floor, reduced to tears, he met deadline after deadline.

May 14th   The room was hot, all the windows were closed. A box was brought in and left on the floor. He hardly moved during the next week, but lay against the wire making a bulge in the netting. Occasionally he would jab his tongue against the wire and lick the mesh with his tongue. . . . After seven days he finally sat up.

May 21st   He sits for a long time staring at the slowly collapsing fire, repeatedly closing his left eye, and swivelling his right eye inwards and upwards, as far to the left as possible.

May 22nd   He walked for some distance down the river bank.

He moved from one museum to another.

He walks through an oppressively warm system of tunnels. These tunnels had originally been sealed off to form a vacuum, but over the years have become filled with the breath of a million people. He walks carefully between rows of sleeping rats. . . . In the walls of the tunnels are tanks filled with water, in which swim conger eels, perch, bream, barbel, roach, electric eels and dace. In a tank of its own swims the largest carp, which had eventually been dragged from the lake only after wedging itself in underwater brambles. The carp is now bleached pink. Several tanks contain only weed.

May 24th   His condition was a seven inch knife.

May 25th   Someone shouted and a chase began.

He turns and runs from the cloud of hairs blowing off the bushes that surround the lake by the railway.

May 26th They slowly circle to one side and shoot him through the lungs from a broadside position. They crouch beside the body, check the eyes, and drag the body into the sunlight and manoeuvre it so that the blood from the external wounds drains away on the sloping ground. They sit down on the ground beside the body, smoke cigarettes and talk quietly until the bleeding has virtually stopped, then they roll him onto his back, unsheath their knives and begin to gut him. First they cut off his testicles and slice the penis away from the belly to its root. They tie a hard knot in the penis, so that no bladder fluid will seep out. They make incisions in the groin and cut round the entire area closely surrounding the knotted penis and the anal opening, so that this section only remains connected to the tubes and ducts that emerge through the pelvic opening. They also cut away the small wedge of muscle tissue which lies between the penis and the anus. They stop for a few minutes, take off their jackets and roll up their sleeves, and then return to their work. Starting about three inches forward of the pelvis one of the men carefully splits the belly a couple of inches, and pushes the first two fingers of his left hand into the opening with the palm turned down. He then inserts his knife at the fork between his fingers, blade edge up, and begins to cut, the fingers travelling ahead of the blade, pressing the intestines away from the blade so that they will not be cut or punctured. When he reaches the ribs he removes his guiding fingers, and taking hold of the knife handle with both hands rips right up through the chest, clear to the throat at the base of the head. Now he splits straight down through the muscle between the legs, exposing the pelvic plate, and the whole torso is open from groin to throat. The other man amputates the left forearm, which he hands to his partner who uses it to hammer the knife through the pelvic bone, until the pelvic plate has been cut across its entire length. The two men roll up their jackets; one man lifts up the cut body by the legs while the other man places the jackets as a cushion beneath the buttocks. They kneel side by side between the thighs. They grip a leg each and press them apart, bracing their shoulders against the inside of the knees until the pelvic arch is broken. They remove their jackets from under the body and rest for a few minutes, before manoeuvring the body until it lies sideways across the

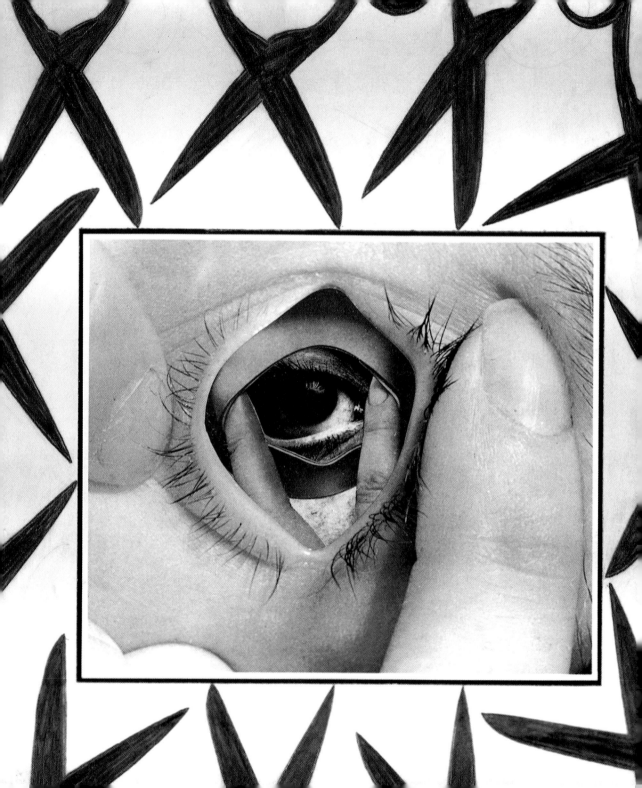

sloping ground, allowing a few large clots of blood to fall out of the chest cavity. They return to their work, taking it in turns to cut loose first the gullet, then the heart and lungs, then the diaphragm and all attached organs, until all the entrails are removed and roll away down the slope. They then wipe out the inside of the torso, and also their own hands, arms and knives. One man turns the gutted body over onto its belly and pumps the legs up and down, massaging the limbs with his hands, while the other man trims the heart and liver from the unwanted viscera and places them in a small plastic bag, which he places in his pocket. He then puts on his jacket and walks out of the garden to the telephone kiosk across the street. He returns and tells his companion that he has phoned for the van. They sit down, light cigarettes and wait.

HER

He left her crying. Five minutes later he returned for his cigarettes; she was still crying. He left again. His smile ran on rails. Light orchestral music filled the railway station. With his ticket between his teeth he moved to the front of the train.

The soliders on the train had all been issued with ball-point pens, and they had learned to click them in unison to a simple rhythm. All the soldiers in the carriage clicked their pens, laughing as they sustained the rhythm, and hooting at any one who missed a click.

"Out in the open . . . just one local girl in a button-up dress who wouldn't stop when instructed . . . chased her into an iron gate . . . in the headlights she gets spread . . . the back of her neck rubbed against the wall . . . mud smeared on the inside of her cheek . . . banknotes glued to her hair."

"Now let me tell you one . . . 'A candle-lit meal . . . when she had eaten as much as she could she gave a little cough . . . she felt in the pocket of her dress; there was something hard inside. She pulled out a diamond and a pearl, and a ruby that she had picked up . . . she was bent over backwards . . . she spent most of the night in this position . . . her mother and sisters were on their hands and knees . . . put one hand on her stomach and one on her back . . . stepped up and down on a chair . . . bound to a damask couch with chains around her ankles . . . her mother and sisters did press-ups on an orange mattress . . . her mouth had long strings . . . eyelids sellotaped back . . . skirt rigid . . . sponges in her mouth were sprayed with liquid chocolate . . . swung around the room . . . across the refrigerator . . . through the wallpaper came the sound of the sea . . .' "

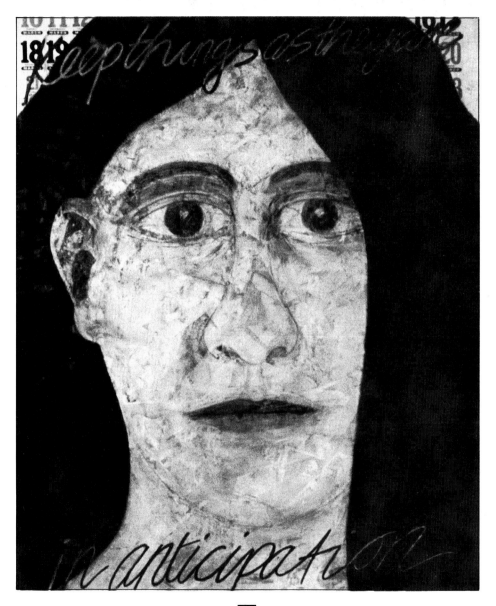

REPERTORY

R epertory : a series of imagined presentations in a locked and empty theatre.
The theatre has the conventional proscenium arch and raked auditorium.
Each evening presentation lasts one hour.

MONDAY
The curtain is down. The footlights are on, the houselights are dimmed.

TUESDAY
The curtain is down. The footlights are on, the houselights dimmed. In front of each chair in the orchestra pit is a music stand; on each music stand is an open score. Large moths settle on the sheets of music.

WEDNESDAY
The curtain is up. The footlights are on, the houselights dimmed. The set is a 1930's domestic interior: sofa, deep armchairs, glass fronted bookshelves around the walls, a standard-lamp which is on, a portrait of an old man with white hair in a gilt frame, a talking budgerigar in a cage.

THURSDAY
The curtain is up, the houselights dimmed. The scene is set for a banquet. Miniature portions of charcoal-grilled meats are set out on long trestle tables; also a variety of fish, raw vegetables in strips, freshly pulped tomato, cheeses, spiced meat balls, several kinds of olives, stuffed vine leaves, bread envelopes

containing shredded lettuce, cucumbers covered with yoghourt; all in darkness. A single spotlight illuminates the lobster salad.

FRIDAY

The curtain is up. The footlights are on, the houselights dimmed. The whole stage is covered with brass vases filled with roses.

SATURDAY

The curtain is up. The houselights are dimmed. All stage-lights, spots and arc lamps are on full. The scene is a modern domestic interior. On the top of the television, on the top of the radio, on the coffee-table, in the fire grate, in the coal bucket, on the typewriter, on the inflatable sofa and on the black leather chairs are slabs of butter; the butter melts.

SUNDAY

The curtain is up. The footlights are on, the houselights dimmed. The stage-set is a "contemporary living-room". The walls of the room are white embossed; on the wall is a brass framed mirror; on the corner of the mirror a stuffed canary is perched. The ceiling is white embossed, the carpet green with a yellow floral pattern. Grey, nylon covered chairs; black, yellow and green nylon-fur cushions. On the wall a pair of brass bellows on which is a side view of a galleon hangs from a hook in the shape of a front view of a galleon. On the mantelpiece is a hat-shaped clock, a bell-shaped musical box, a swan-shaped flowerpot, and two empty candlesticks. On the brown carved sideboard, brown carved table, white painted window ledge and veneered cocktail cabinet are white vases filled with paper flowers. Every quarter of an hour the doors of the cuckoo-clock burst open and the cuckoo springs out making its noise.

MONDAY

The curtain is up. The footlights are on, the houselights dimmed. Onstage is an old aeroplane.

TUESDAY

The curtain is up. The footlights are on, the houselights dimmed. Onstage a tethered dog walks round in circles.

WEDNESDAY

The curtain is up. The footlights are dimmed, the houselights dimmed. Onstage is a small illuminated fish tank in which a big grey carp swims backwards and forwards.

THURSDAY

The curtain is up. The footlights are on, the houselights dimmed. Onstage is a sunken swimming pool, illuminated from below and filled with blue water. Around the swimming pool stand stuffed sheep.

FRIDAY

The curtain is up. The footlights are dimmed, the houselights dimmed. Onstage, spotlights illuminate an indoor show-jumping arena. Overlooking the arena green tarpaulin covers a structure ten metres tall, like a one-fingered glove.

SATURDAY

The curtain is up. The footlights are on, the houselights dimmed. Onstage is a three-metre white cube which moves fifty centimetres upstage during one hour.

SUNDAY

The curtain is up. The footlights are on, the houselights dimmed. Upstage, in a line close to the footlights stand wooden toy animals on wheels: dogs, cats, horses, cows, zebras, lions and tigers; their shadows fall on the white backdrop at the rear of the stage.

MONDAY

The curtain is up. The footlights are on, the houselights dimmed. The stage is covered with earth in the middle of which stands a small tree on which a swarm of bees has settled.

TUESDAY

The curtain is up. The footlights are on, the houselights dimmed. The stage is covered with artificial grass on which squirm thousands of earthworms.

WEDNESDAY

The curtain is up. The footlights are dimmed, the houselights dimmed.

BAD WAITERS

Bad waiters shirk their allotted responsibilities.
Bad waiters carry pencils behind their ears.
Bad waiters have a bad form of speech.
Bad waiters have unpolished shoes.
Bad waiters have untrained eyes.
Bad waiters keep teaspoons in their trouser pockets.
Bad waiters talk during the service.
Bad waiters soil menus.
Bad waiters spill soup.
Bad waiters splash sauce.
Bad waiters interrupt.
Bad waiters nudge guests.
Bad waiters simper.
Bad waiters laugh suddenly.
Bad waiters leer.
Bad waiters have filed teeth.
Bad waiters cringe.
Bad waiters stutter.
Bad waiters squint.
Bad waiters stare.
Bad waiters sneer.
Bad waiters giggle.
Bad waiters have bad breath.

Bad waiters have body odour.
Bad waiters have foot smell.
Bad waiters have dandruff.
Bad waiters have oily hands.
Bad waiters have greasy clothes.
Bad waiters scratch pimples.
Bad waiters finger their ears.
Bad waiters pick their noses.
Bad waiters cough and savour the phlegm.
Bad waiters have soiled cuffs.
Bad waiters have soiled socks.
Bad waiters suck their teeth.
Bad waiters clean their fingernails on the corner of the menu.
Bad waiters have open zips.
Bad waiters lean against the walls.
Bad waiters slouch.
Bad waiters sidle.
Bad waiters edge along the walls.
Bad waiters smell the floral decorations.
Bad waiters linger over helping a lady out of her coat.
Bad waiters flex their muscles.
Bad waiters stroke themselves.
Bad waiters have nervous tics.
Bad waiters flick crumbs.
Bad waiters flip coins.
Bad waiters do impersonations.
Bad waiters show their scars.
Bad waiters serve whole ox tongues.
Bad waiters grip wine bottles between their legs.
Bad waiters yell.
Bad waiters squeeze bread.
Bad waiters snap their fingers.
Bad waiters spin plates.

Bad waiters kick open doors.
Bad waiters sneeze on the ice cream.
Bad waiters slobber.
Bad waiters mould butter into ambiguous shapes.
Bad waiters make dubious jokes while serving the oysters.
Absent-minded waiters finger the éclairs.
Rough waiters break the bread over their knees.
Casual waiters pour the custard from a bucket.
Careless waiters piss down their trouser legs while serving the grapes.
Tense waiters cut the gâteau with a karate chop.
Some waiters abuse the wine funnels.
Some waiters soak their dentures on the reception desk.
Sneaky waiters trip up guests.
Unspeakable waiters wipe their noses on guests' ties.
Some waiters, rotten to the core, jerk off into the soup tureen.
Bad waiters give everybody the wrong coats.

FETCH

Aman and a dog are in a field.
The man throws a stick for the dog to fetch.
The dog chases after the stick while the man
jumps into his car behind the nearby hedge
and drives swiftly away.

THE SERMON

It has been the wisdom of the law to keep the mean between the two extremes: of too much stiffness in refusing, and of too much readiness in admitting any variation from it.

On the one side it is but reasonable that after weighty and important consideration, such changes and alterations should be made, as those in position of authority consider either necessary or expedient.

However, on the other side, common experience shows that where change has been made of things advisedly established, with no evident necessity for such change, then many inconveniences have subsequently ensued; and those many times greater than the evils that were intended to be remedied by the change.

And so it is necessary that we acknowledge our manifold sins and wickedness, and that we should not dissemble nor cloak them, but confess them with a lowly, penitent and obedient heart, to the end that we might obtain forgiveness. For we have erred and strayed like lost sheep. We have followed too much the devices and desires of our own hearts. We have offended against the laws. We have left undone those things that we ought to have done, and we have done those things which we ought not to have done. And there is no health in us.

The time is ripe to clarify again those areas in which you may need guidance. Therefore, in cases of partial delivery, when it is unlikely that the child can be completely alive, baptism should be conferred. If the head is born the baptism is certainly valid; if any other limb presents itself baptism should be conferred

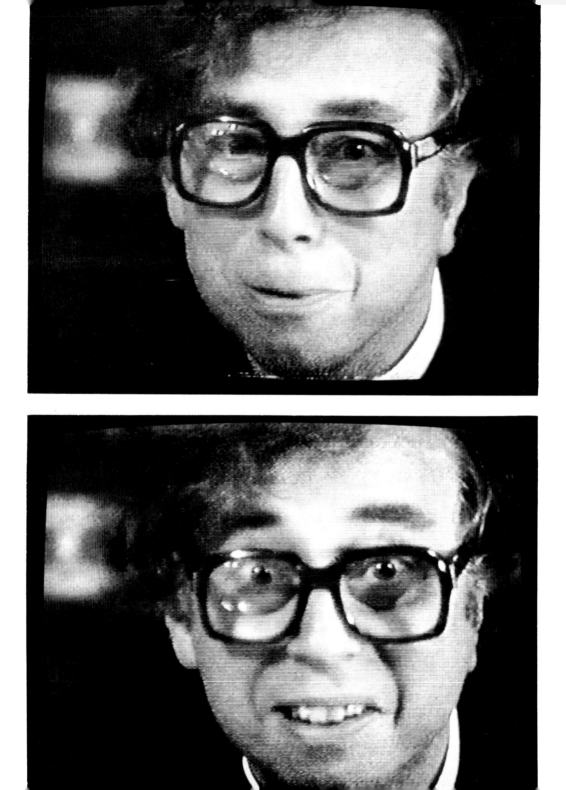

on that member, but as the validity in this case is doubtful, conditional baptism should be given afterwards on the head, even if the child appears to have died meanwhile.

It should be particularly noted that baptism cannot be administered before the membranes are ruptured, and it cannot be administered on the umbilical cord, as this is not a permanent member of the child. It must also be emphasised that membranes must not be ruptured for the purpose of baptising a non-viable foetus.

Therefore, clamp both sides, cut it away and turn up the ends, just enough to insert a gloved finger. If necessary clip it.

But in the case of monsters, baptism should be given conditionally whether they are alive, doubtfully alive, or recently dead.

In the case of multiple monsters, one arm will do just as well as another.

In the case of a mother dying in childbirth while the child is possibly still alive, and a doctor is present who can perform such an operation, then Caesarean section should be performed and the child baptised if in danger of death. If the child is dead or dies immediately afterwards, it should be replaced in the uterus and buried with the mother.

The water must flow and it must flow over the skin. It is not sufficient if it flows only over hair or thick grease.

Extra fingers or toes may be removed, even though they be physically sound. This would not impair the perfect function of the body, but on the contrary might remove potential handicaps at work (for instance, operating machines designed for normal five-fingered hands) and of economic kinds (for instance the necessity of wearing specially fitted shoes), and for the same reasons plastic surgery is quite legitimately employed not only to repair consequences of accidents or illness, but also to correct natural defects.

In the light of these facts then, we have to examine the proposal that the marriage act should be performed with a perforated condom as a method to provide ejaculate for examination without interfering with the sacred act of married love. The use of a condom with holes would allow semen to escape into the vagina and retain only a part for transmission to the laboratory. This will be permissable if the perforations allow by far the largest part of the

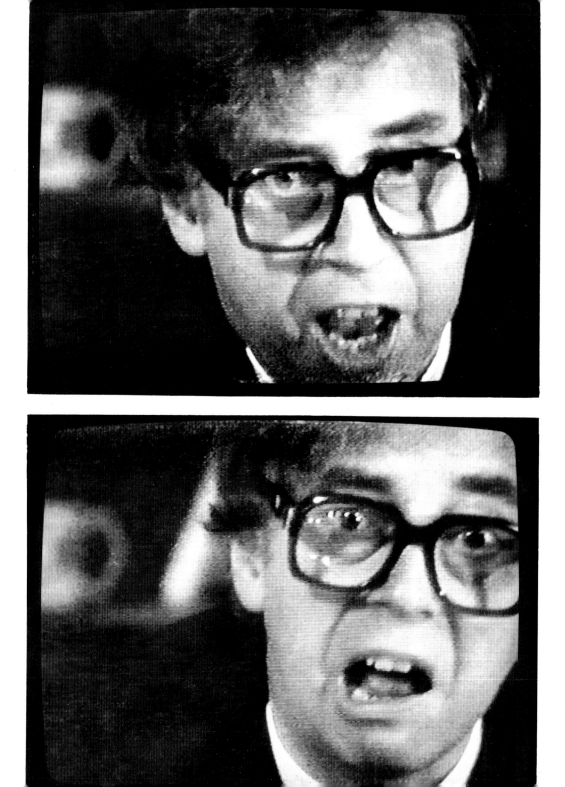

ejaculate to penetrate through them. As only a small amount of semen is necessary for microscopical examination it would be feasible to arrange this, but even so the results would not be satisfactory. The total volume of ejaculate cannot be estimated. Furthermore, while this method makes it possible to observe the appearance of the spermatozoa and the relative percentage of active and inactive forms, to count the number that is active in a specific volume, and how many remain active after twenty-four hours, the rubber of which condoms are made is thought to have some spermicidal action, which falsifies the picture.

Intercourse using a condom with the end cut off would be permissable to direct the semen forward in a case of malformation and thus increase the likelihood of conception.

It is true that masturbation is the method most widely used for obtaining specimens of semen, but this of course is not permissable as it involves the unnatural use of the sexual faculty, divorced from its proper purpose, which is against the natural law. Even from the practical point of view the method is unsatisfactory, because masturbation done half-heartedly frequently does not produce a specimen equal to the ejaculate during the satisfying intercourse with the beloved partner. Once again we see how the law and good medical practice concur. The only explanation possible for the continued use of this method is its simplicity, particularly for the laboratory.

You may well ask for how long you should practice. There is no answer to this question. The length of time you can yield yourself to yourself depends entirely upon the permission you are granted.

Slacken all your muscles. Allow yourself to drop. Let go. Drift. Sink like a child without fear. With legs and feet parallel, curl the toes.

Relax — squeeze the balls — relax.

Point toes — relax — squeeze the balls — relax.

Rotate feet outwards — curl the toes — relax — squeeze the balls — relax.

In rotated position — point toes — relax — squeeze the balls — relax.

Rotate feet inwards — curl the toes — relax — squeeze the balls — relax.

Return to parallel position — tighten knees — relax — squeeze the balls —relax.

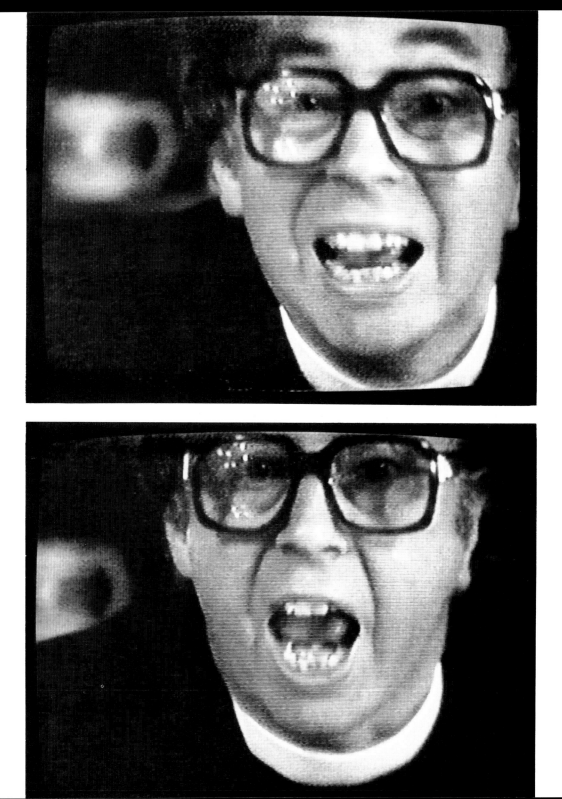

Tighten thighs — relax.

From now on it is understood that you will squeeze the balls and relax after each new contraction.

Practice this manoeuvre each hour of the day.

Keep the house free from flies.

Burn valueless papers, flowers, magazines, toys, loose floor coverings, hangings, tablecloths, upholstered furniture, ottomans, books, small objects which are not required, highly polished furniture, all unnecessary ornaments.

For original sin is the fault and corruption of the nature of every man, for man is very far gone from original righteousness, and is of his own nature inclined to evil, so that the flesh lusts always contrary to the spirit, and therefore in every person born into this world it deserves the law's condemnation.

And this infection of nature remains, because the lust of the flesh, which some call wisdom, some sensuality, some the affection, some the desire of the flesh, is not subject to the law. For lust of the flesh has of itself the nature of sin.

And the wicked amongst us, even though they may visibly press with their teeth the bread of the law, yet in no way are they believers in the law.

And to that wicked man, that devil in our midst, I say to that man:

You Dirty, Filthy, Pig! You should have Cancer! Eating your Body away you Scum! Lepers are cleaner than you, they can be healed! You spread your Filth to the Innocent, you are the Pig on the Filthy Woman! You Skunk! I hope you never close your eyes in Sleep! You Beast! Skunk! All you can do is warp your own Mind in Filth, Scum, Horror, unbelievable Muck! You should crawl on your Filthy Nude Belly the rest of your life! The Dirt from your Nose is too good for you to Eat! If you were smitten with Boils like Job I would Rejoice! Swine! Scum of a Whore's stinking Womb! Reptile! Garbage! Lower than Mud! You have poisoned our Children with your Filth you Reeking Swine! Bastard son of a Bastard father, may your Children be born Blind, may your Filthy Wife be Poisoned by her own Juice! The Hovel you call your Home should burn to the Ground and you burn slowly in it! And if Lightning split your Chest or Hail broke your head it would be less than you deserve! Slime!

Reeking Slime! You should be Gutted! Your Stomach torn out while you Watch! Eye for Eye, Tooth for Tooth, Hand for Hand, Foot for Foot! Burning for Burning, Wound for Wound, Stripe for Stripe! Snake! Snake-Slime! Your own Excrement, may it Suffocate you! Your own Vomit, may it Choke you! Your own Urine, may you Drown in it! Burnt Alive! Your Eyes torn out ! Your Nostrils stuffed with Pus! Your Face rubbed in your own Pig Filth! You Filthy Swine! Your Hair should turn white with Plague! Your whole Body covered with Burning Sores! And I would Laugh! Ha! Ha! At those Yellow Spots, those Weeping Scabs! Scrape them Off! Ha! Ha! Scrape them Off! As I laugh! Laugh as you tear your Filthy Flesh! You Twisted Swine! Whoever touches you should Wash their Clothes! Hand for Hand, Foot for Foot! You Swine! You Filthy Swine! God made Heaven and Earth and all that in there is and He never forgot a thing! He does not pay His Debts in Money! No! It is Too Late! Too Late for you, you Dirty, Filthy Pig!

MEMORY LANE

Y ou end life as you began it: doubly incontinent. You are put on the pot and taken off. You are treated like a child. But you are not a child. You may not appear wise, but wisdom, or at least experience, may be buried beneath the accumulated rust. The tape-heads are corroded, they need cleaning, they will never again be as good as they were, everything wears out, but they still play. The sound is distorted, the balance wrong, there's too much surface noise, but the content may still be there. But what content? You can count to twenty, or twenty back to one? You can remember which monarch was on the throne in 1916, or 1926, or 1946? You saw their pictures in the papers? You stood on the pavement and waved your flag? Or did not. You held your flag firmly by your side? You would like the royal car to crash? You would like to see the rich bitch burnt alive? But you used to have wet dreams about her. No, I don't remember. Ask me another. The General Strike? Ah yes, the General Strike, I remember it well, it was in all the papers. What's that? A train. Well I used to drive a train, I was a train driver, that's what I wanted to be at school, Hugh Mydellton Infants, my father was a train driver before me, and when there was the General Strike some toffee-nosed student from University drove my bleeding train. If I could only meet him now, I'd throttle the bastard, weak as I am, so help me I'd throttle him! But can you remember what year that was? No. 1926? No, I can't remember, but I can see their faces now, those fresh pink faces and blue eyes, walking towards the engine sheds, and him there, him in the brand new overalls still with the creases across the legs, that fresh-faced bastard there was going to drive my train! I was never in the papers. No, I tell a

lie, I was once: Silver Wedding, Islington Gazette. Poor Mavis. Poor sod. No one should die like that. I said for pity's sake doctor, put her down. Give her something so she won't wake up. But it's no good, they won't listen, and how do you get the pills if you haven't got the education? I swear I would have done away with her myself, I'd have put her head in the oven if I'd known it would be like that. I cried. I don't mind admitting I cried like a baby. I punched the wall. Fetched all the skin off my knuckles. It was the year of the Coronation.

DEAR SON

Dear Son,

My letter has just been interrupted, Eric at the shop wanted to know if your father would be in as he was going to help him polish the car. I explained the situation so that's bad luck, it's not often that anyone offers to help with cleaning a car. Your father is about the same, quite alert but not a very good colour. It is very difficult visiting really, he can hear OK and understands what you are saying but he cannot answer at all although he tries hard to speak and makes a noise and believes he is saying the words properly but it is always the same funny sound. It's starting to rain so cheerio and I hope I'll hear from you soon.

Love Mother.

Dear Son,

Well you certainly had some news in your letter. This week has passed rather quickly and the weather is cold and bright. Last Thursday the doorbell went and on Friday morning we bumped into your Auntie Doris, she was going to buy a carpet from the department store as this week is two shillings in the £ off purchases and apparently she would be getting about fifteen shillings back. Yesterday there was a knock at the door and the little girl from across the road went running along to school, thank goodness that was solved. On Sunday we went to see your father and he will not get up again in my estimation. We have to do all the talking as he can only make noises and then gets exhausted, he flops in his bed and hasn't wanted to get up at all so I think he is resigning himself to the fact, that seems to me the outlook. On the way back there was a car horn sounding behind us and it was some old friends we hadn't seen for years. I am now going to have my hair done so I'll say goodbye.

Love Mother.

Dear Son,
How good it was to hear from you again you certainly sound busy. Yesterday Mrs Thompson was going to buy a new coat, so I went with her and as well as her buying one, you can guess, I bought one as well. It is an off-white and blue check with a suede collar and buttons, it doesn't need any alteration. Do you remember your old Aunt Mary who used to live in the bungalow by the river and now lives in town, her husband's name is Eric? Anyway there was a news item in the evening paper on Saturday where a woman's coat and shoes were found on the river bank and a statement by a man who had seen a woman walk into the river and Eric has identified the clothes as belonging to Mary, the police are still searching for the body. And Mrs Weston who lived at the hardware shop was electrocuted last week by a do-it-yourself job that a relative had done for her, and she was only forty-eight so she didn't live long after her husband. So it has been quite a week. All the best as always, I must close now, hoping to see you soon.

Love Mother.

Dear Son,
It was nice to get your letter. I thought the snaps were very good. I've had the old shed taken down and a new one put up, it looks very nice alongside the coalhouse, it's got glass all round, everyone says it's a big improvement. Oscar and Ethel set off on their holidays last Tuesday but they had to return home because Oscar's memory is not very good, it's sad to hear some of the things he says. Stuart and Margaret are coming round for their dinner tomorrow instead of a birthday party because we couldn't get sixty-two candles on the cake. I'm going to have a bath so I'll say goodbye for now.

Love Mother.

P.S. Uncle Henry has a burst ulcer.

Dear Son,

Just received your card and had a smile to myself. I don't like cycling anymore, I'm better walking but I keep slipping down. I saw Princess Anne's wedding in colour on Ethel's TV but I wish I could have seen it down in London. I would have camped out on the pavement, we never get anything like that round here. Stuart came round yesterday and concreted the floor of the shed and put big posts up all round the garden, your Dad would have been pleased to see what he really can do. I've got your Dad on my mind just lately, I keep thinking of that terrible July three years ago, so I've kept busy to try to forget it. I've painted the kitchen white and blue and had the bathroom done blue and white and the ceiling tiled, its a complete change. Well I must close now and get my hair washed. I'm looking forward to my trip to London, I've saved some beef coupons so don't buy a joint I'll bring one.

Love Mother.

Dear Son,

Hope you are quite well and enjoying life. I've just come back from Borrowash, I've been for my dinner and I must say it was very nice. By the way I've received my £10 for the aged, what about that? Your Uncle Oscar died on Monday, it was a blessing for your Auntie Ethel, she was about to crack up herself. He was buried on Wednesday and they asked me to follow. I've had a nice suite made in olive green with yellow cushions, it looks lovely in the middle of the room. It's rained all day and it's St. Swithin's so let's hope it's not true. Now I'm going to have a bath and go to bed so I'll have to say goodbye.

Love Mother.

P.S. What about the Olympic Games?

Dear Son,

Just a short note to tell you your Auntie Alice fell over. She was standing on a chair, one of those little boudoir chairs, she was putting up the decorations when she fell off. She hit the wall twice. She was upside down at the bottom of the stairs when they found her. Had to have eight stitches. That's the way things seem to be nowadays, up one minute down the next. But did you read in the paper about how in Mexico the cemetery officials dug up a hundred and fourteen bodies because the relatives were behind with payments on the plots? I'm glad we settled up quickly on your Dad's, we don't want anything like that here. That big bomb that went off must have been very near to you, are you alright?

Love Mother.

Dear Son,
How nice to hear from you. Grandad was cremated on Tuesday and everyone came back to our house. I go on holiday a week today, it gets a bit boring on my own sometimes, I'm already looking at holiday brochures for October. The nights are getting lighter and the bulbs are coming up in the garden, and I'm busy saving for my holidays so I'll have to say cheerio.

Love Mother.

Dear Son,
Just a line to let you know I got back safe. I liked my sea trip but Mrs Childs was sick all the way there and back, it's put her off. I'm tired after my holiday, there was such a lot to see, but we were taken to each place by bus so we didn't get wet. It was a nice little holiday, I'm ready for another. Time to go swimming so I'll say cheerio.

Love Mother.

Dear Son,
Thanks for the birthday card it was very nice, I like scenes. I just hope this weather changes I'm sick of it. I've been out in the garden though every minute between the showers, I've planted all round the edge. The back garden our Stuart's been doing, and you know him he hired a bulldozer and he's dug it all up, he loves anything like that. One day it was six o'clock and I said to him have you had your tea and he said I haven't had my breakfast yet, you wouldn't think he was the same lad would you? And every morning he's up at five sawing down elm trees that have got the disease, he never stops, but their new stove just eats it. The kettle's boiling so I'll stop now.

Love Mother.

Dear Son,

We've had the floods here for two weeks, it's only just cleared up. I was stuck in the house for five days. And when you get desperate and you search the house for a box of chocolates that's when you can't find one. You search here and there and high and low and you think I'm sure I put one away for a rainy day, but can you find it? No. And your mouth starts to water and you think I'd give anything for a nice chocolate with a soft centre. Looking out of the window doesn't help either. First night after the water had gone down I'd just gone to bed and there was a knock on the wall. Rap-rap-rap. It was her next door, the zip of her dress was stuck and she couldn't get out of it. And only yesterday she knocked, she couldn't get her oven to work. She'd had a meal cooked for her and brought to her, all she had to do was heat it up but she couldn't work the switch on the oven, she should be in a home. Did you go to the cricket? I often watch the television to see if I can see you in the crowd. Sometimes I'm sure I can.

Love Mother.

Dear Son,

Harry Bradshaw dropped dead on his holidays in Bournemouth. Not a single Labour man got in at the council elections. Harry never came out of the house for a week, you know how he used to stand at the gate going "Good morning. Good morning," well not for a week was he seen, it preyed on his mind, and the next thing you know he's dead. There was to be a surprise for him when he got back home from holiday, a portrait of him in his mayor's robes and golden chain on the wall in the front room in an oak frame, and a great big flower arrangement underneath, but he never lived to see it, what a waste. Still, they'll be able to think of him every time they look at the wall. A lot of top show I think. And the funeral was a lavish affair with all the trimmings, it's a pity he missed it. Anyway I thought you'd like to know.

Love Mother.

Dear Son,

Just thought I'd drop you a line to see if your boil went down? They're nasty things boils, always ran in the family on your father's side you know. Last Tuesday there was a face at the living room window, it was a woman about sixty years old with a very tanned face. She shouted, 'Are there any men in there?' I said, 'No they're round the back.' I don't know why I said that because there aren't any round the back either, but you can't be too sure there's some funny folk about nowadays. Anyway that was the last I saw of her. Stuart's just arrived with half a pig so we won't go short this week.

Love Mother.

Dear Son,

How long will this weather last? It's a wonder we haven't all been had up for being improperly dressed. Margaret tells me that Stuart has been walking around in just his pants for over a week now. It must be hot in London. I often think of you in the middle of all that meat, do you ever get any cheap? By the way, there was big excitement at the store where your Auntie Doris works last Friday morning. They had been burgled during the night. The police think they had been in from ten o'clock at night to five in the morning. All the wages, cigarettes and perfume were taken, and whole rails of sheepskin coats. There were two big holes in the strongroom door. There were chicken bones and sweet wrappers scattered all over the place. Apparently it was a right mess. They even did their business on a pile of children's anoraks. How is your cooking getting on?

Love Mother.

Dear Son,

We've got the greenflies something terrible up here. You can't go out. I've never seen anything like it. I'm keeping all the windows shut but it gets on your nerves with it being so hot and muggy, you sit inside puthering you can hardly breathe, but you daren't open the door or else they all swarm inside. They settle all over you and get into everything. They're all over the window now, but you should see this, there's three steamrollers going past one after the other and all the cars are stuck behind, the drivers look like thunder. I'm glad I'm not one of them. And talk about neighbours, them next door their fuchsia died, they can't seem to grow a thing. So I went up to see your Uncle Cyril, I said Cyril how much will you take for one of your fuchsias? I got it for 15p. Then I went round and knocked on next door and said now then I've come to dig up that dead fuchsia, I've got you another. They stood there gormless. Anyroad, I dug a hole and stuck it in and now it's flowering. They said isn't it wonderful, we can't believe it, we're going to call it Dennis, they talk to it you know. Who do you think will win the election?

Love Mother.

Dear Son,
I went and did a daft thing. I dropped a paving stone on my foot. They put a plaster on my foot, a great big ugly thing. When I came back from the hospital I couldn't eat for two days I felt so sick. Then the third day I crawled on my hands and knees through to the kitchen and into the pantry. Well of course I couldn't carry anything back into the living room I had to eat it there, and I found some bread, some celery in a jug of water and some butter hard as a rock, it was perishing cold I had to cut the butter like cake it wouldn't spread, so I sliced the butter, sliced the cheese, cut the bread and made a sandwich and ate it with the celery, it tasted beautiful. Then I mashed a pot of tea and I felt much better. But having the toilet upstairs was my biggest bugbear. For two days I had to croodle down over a bucket in the kitchen, that's how I managed. Only on the fourth day did I let Stuart know what had happened and he came round and finished the path, it was those paving stones your Dad bought me for my birthday just before he went into hospital that last time, they'd stood in the backyard since then. I think I'll do some baking so take care.

Love Mother.

Dear Son,

Excuse card, I've run out of writing paper and envelopes. I'll be better when I get my plaster off next week. I've got cold sores all around my mouth and a runny nose. I'm writing this in bed on my knee while drinking a cup of tea. Sorry the pants were too small, you must be getting fat.

Love Mother.

P.S. I joined the Red Cross.

Dear Son,

You remember you were asking how your cousin Trevor was, well your Auntie Doreen is still pushing him around in a push chair, it's like pushing a big man. Because you know when he sees me his arms start going and he's staring and shouting. And then he gets nasty and he starts pushing his finger against his nose and going, "Eyup! Eyo! Laffinat! Laffinat!," he's picked that up from me because I used to say to him what are you laughing at? And he still pushes his finger against his nose and Doreen says, 'You know what he's saying, he's saying we're nosy, well the other day this woman took it badly and I nearly got her by the throat, you've got to make allowance, but I can't stand another day like today, another day like today and I'm going to do away with myself,' that's what Doreen says. You can't blame her, what a burden, I thank my lucky stars you and Stuart were all right. There's someone at the door so I'll have to go.

Love Mother.

Dear Son,

It was a surprise to get your card. You certainly gad about. Stuart's business is thriving, he's done very well just lately. You remember all that weevilled egg powder he got stuck with, couldn't sell it anywhere except to the maggot factory and then it killed all the flies? Even the dogs wouldn't eat it. It was no good for anything and he'd got thirty-two tons of it. Well eventually he sold it to a nuclear power station in Scotland, they use it for protein membrane between metal plates, it's the best thing for the job apparently, they can't get enough of it. And he even found a use for those forty-two thousand first world war mule boots. He put glass tops on them and sold them as ash trays, you'll see them in all the fancy furnishing shops soon. His other current lines are split baked beans, cloudy apple juice, chocolate bars with the corners knocked off, and ground nut oil. He had a bit of bother with that corned beef, you might have read about it in the papers. But he's doing very well with pigs tails, pigs masks and pigs trotters in tins, all packed in white fat, they're very popular with the blacks. And he sold those six hundred swiss rolls which had got mould on, to the hunt for the hounds at the kennels. Stuart says after two weeks of eating them they aren't half ready for a fox. Let me know what you want for your birthday.

Love Mother.

Dear Son,
I'm back from my holiday. It was a lovely camp. Proper breakfast, smashing dinner and a very nice tea every day. I won the Fancy Dress, I went as Miss Sandybeach, I was a bathing beauty. I wore my best bathers but I thought the scars on my leg might upset some of them so me and Mrs Plackett made garlands out of crêpe paper like a hula-hula girl but down to my knees. You see I was afraid of slipping again on the dance floor, it was polished like a mirror. So I wore my sandals. You should have seen me, they took polaroids. Out there under the bright lights I trembled like a leaf. It was all done on a clapometer and I came first. My picture should be in the local paper, they are sending it on. A great big meat fly has just flown into the room, just wait a minute while I get rid of it. That's seen it off. Now where was I? Oh yes, the brush. Did you get it safe? I wrapped it up in cardboard and put it in a box so it should have been alright but you never can tell. Well, tomorrow they come to install the telephone, so I'll be able to telephone you instead of writing. So I'll say goodbye until then. Goodbye.

Love Mother.

THE ARTIST'S DREAM

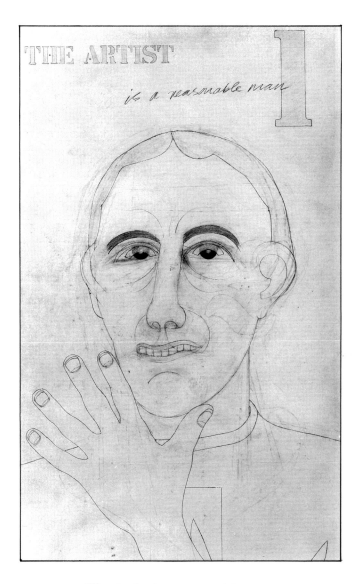

The Artist is a reasonable man.

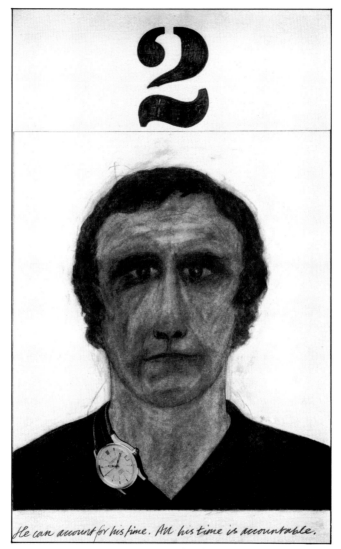

He can account for his time.
All his time is accountable.

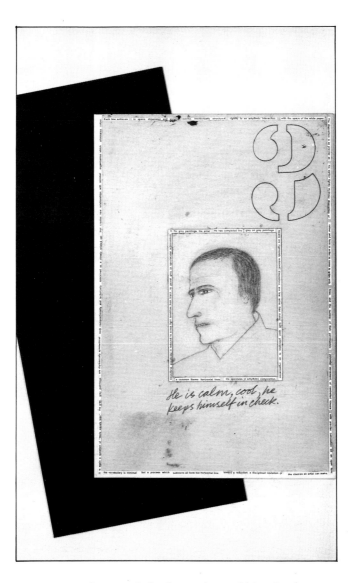

He is calm, cool, he keeps himself in check.

He is demonstrably not odd, though he cultivates minor eccentricities, for he is
constantly aware of his public image.

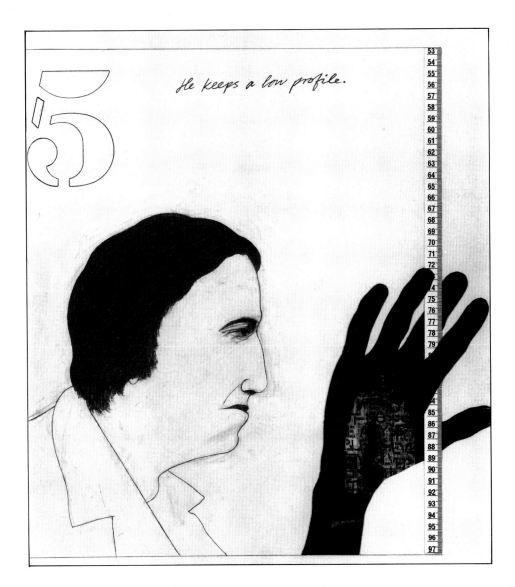

He keeps a low profile.

He is a serious person.

His world is his studio. It is a world of logic, rationalism, aesthetic niceties, pure forms.

His world is his studio. It is a world of logic, rationalism, aesthetic niceties, pure forms.

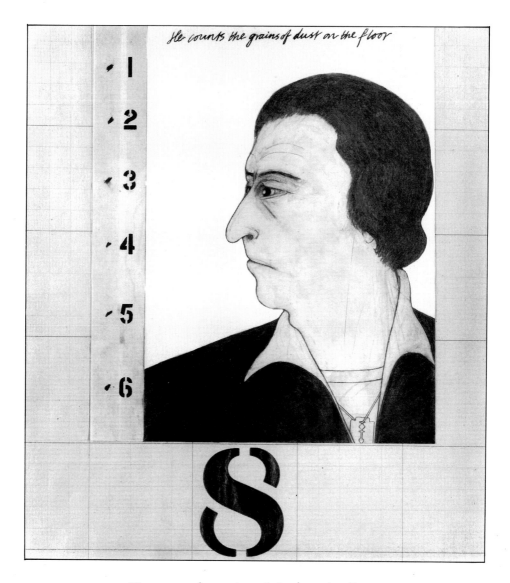

He counts the grains of dust on the floor.

He has a system.

He mistrusts love, desire, magic, emotional
disturbance, convulsive laughter or tears.

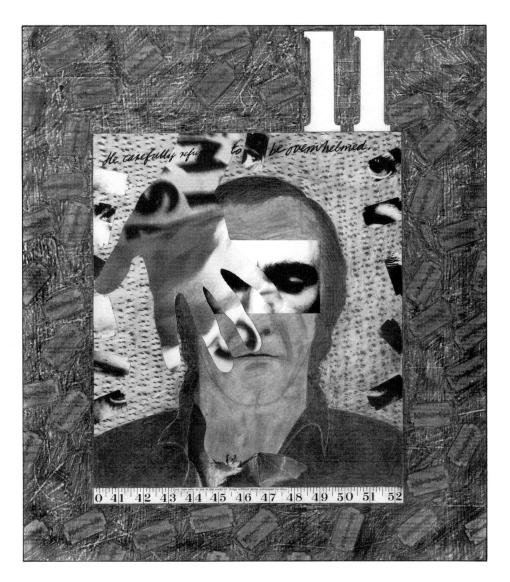

He carefully refuses to be overwhelmed.

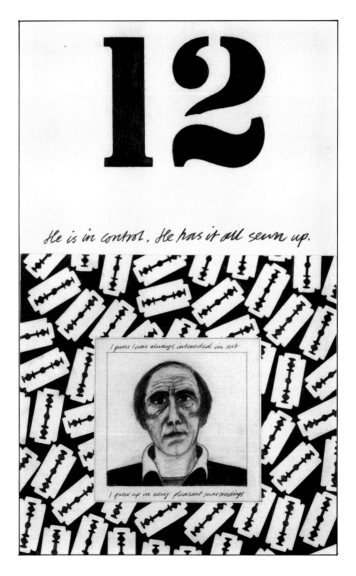

He is in control. He has it all sewn up.

But at the end of his day of nice decisions he reluctantly lies down.
The night hours pass in fitful sleep as he strives to maintain his rational grip.
For at night, in his dreams, the sleep of reason begets monsters.
    It begins with the tap – tap – tap of a little hammer on a metal pipe.
An aperture opening and shutting.
A tethered dog pacing backwards and forwards on the rooftop.
The lift cable stretched.
Stones in the pillow.
Eyeballs rubbing against their sockets.
The rats scratching behind the doors.
A siren in the distance.
Face muscles twitching.
A coiled spring.
Hair shirt.
The skin stretched tight over the cheekbones and across the shoulderblades.
The head an onion being peeled layer by layer.
The toes move independently of one another.
The fingers clench.
The hands reach for the chin.
The teeth bite; the breath hissing through the gaps.
The elbows flap like a bird's wings.
The legs kick.
The knees hit the ribcage.
The body throws itself from side to side.
Sweat runs into the wide open eyes.
Splitting hairs.
Rapid spasms.
Throat closing up.
Beating the head against a brick wall.
Needles stuck in the legs.
Walking barefoot on iron keys.
Climbing a ladder of swords.
Scraped.

The insides of the thighs rubbed with sandpaper.
Hit with sticks.
Alphabet letters raining down.
Lost in a landscape of words; harsh, black and white, stretching to the horizon.
Balls of words like fists roll down the hills.
An avalanche.
Running.
Fighting for breath.
Gasping.
An iron band around the neck.
Mouth filled with razorblades.
Chest and throat choked.
The walls bulge.
Splintering glass.
Droplets falling from a tiny rent, the edges finally torn wide apart.
Beyond the doors the sound of screaming Chinese with electric drills.
Run for your life.
Full tilt.
   Slowing down now.
The spasms subside.
A dull ache from head to toe.
Numb.
Arms heavy as lead.
Weights attached to the fingertips.
His breath fills the room.
Counting sheep.
1 – 2 – 3 – 4
1 – 2 – 3 – 4 – 5
1 – 2 – 3 – 4 – 5 – 6
1 – 2 – 3 – 4 – 5 – 6 – 7
1 – 2 – 3 – 4 – 5 – 6 – 7 – 8
The sheep line up to jump over the fence and are torn to pieces by a pack of stray dogs: Labradors, Airedales, Beagles, Pugs, Sealyhams, Poodles, Spaniels,

Collies, Dachshunds, Great Danes, Corgis, Saint Bernards, Deerhounds, Salukis, Bloodhounds, Pekinese, Border Terriers, Alsatians, Otterhounds, Boxers, Dalmatians, Chows, Bulldogs, Schnauzers, Bedlington Terriers, Afghan Hounds, Samoyeds, Borzois, Golden Retrievers, Red Setters, Fox Terriers, Basset Hounds, Harriers, Border Terriers, Appenzal Mountain Dogs, Jack Russells, Basenjis, Greyhounds, Boston Terriers, Doberman Pinschers, Bullmastiffs, Pointers, Dandie Dinmonts, and lapping up the puddles of blood: a little Chihuahua.

THE NEWS

No LETTERS
Police were called to a post box in Wilson Avenue on Friday and discovered that the post box was empty.

HOUSE ENTERED
A house was entered in Makepeace Drive on Wednesday. The front door had been left unlocked.

HOLE WAS NOT A HOLE
After reporting to the borough council that a hole in Ash Grove needed filling, the parish council heard last week that the hole is in fact a bump. The council will re-report the matter.

STILE NEEDS RESITING
The parish council debated last night whether to contact the owner of the land on which there is a stile on footpath number 4. Opinion was divided, some members saying that the stile was "a trap", others that it was "difficult" but not "impassable".

ELDERLY GET UP AND LEAVE BEFORE THE END
To avoid any discourtesy to the people who are entertaining them, a vote of thanks should be given during the programme and not at the end, members of the Old People's Welfare Committee decided last week.

They agreed that it "looked bad" when elderly people in the audience got up and left before the entertainers had been properly thanked. Councillor Place stated, "I would like to put the record straight on this." He explained that there had been problems with the central heating boiler at the premises. Unfortunately the choir which was providing the entertainment finished its programme while he and the person who was to thank them were in the cloakroom looking at the boiler.

"Everything suddenly stopped. By the time we got back everyone started to get up and everything was in turmoil. There was no chance to give a public vote of thanks. It was chaos."

Councillor Bettles agreed, "This does happen. They get up, start putting their coats on and walk out. For someone who does not expect it this appears to be rude. I think the awkward attitude of some of the old people appears to be the trouble."

SEAT IN SUN NOT TO BE RESITED
The borough council will not resite a seat in the market place, the parish council heard last week. The borough council pointed out that the seat faced in a southerly direction for maximum sunlight and that concrete slabs had been laid in front and under the seat. Councillor Braggs said that many old people had complained of the sun beating down on their heads and that the seat had become "highly unpopular".

NO COMMENT ON LAWN
The parish council is unlikely to make any comment on the increasing size of the lawn at 23 Spinney Road.

MISUSE OF PEDESTRIAN CROSSING BY ELDERLY
Elderly people are crossing zebra crossings in a "devil-may-care manner". That was the opinion of Councillor Atherton at Thursday's meeting of the community council. He said that he had been compelled to pull back one elderly pedestrian by the coat.

HIS GARDEN IS BEING USED AS A THOROUGHFARE: SHOULD HE BE TOLD?

The parish council last week voted against telling the owner of a house on Wilmot Road that his garden was being used as a thoroughfare. Voting was 5 to 4 against with one abstention.

SWIMMING POOL A DISGRACE

At Thursday's meeting of the town council, Councillor Webb said that the condition of the town swimming pool was "a disgrace". Grass was growing through the tiles and six or seven inches of stagnant water lay in the pool. Councillor Bates said that it was because the pool was underused.

CHIP PAN FIRE

Firemen were called to a chip pan fire at 87 Orchard Street on Sunday, but the blaze was out when they arrived.

WASTE OF ELECTRICITY

The parish council is to call in an energy expert regarding the apparent waste of electricity through keeping street lights lit late at night.

REINSTATEMENT OF GRASS VERGE

The reinstatement of a grass verge at Harrington Avenue is to be pressed for by the parish council as a matter of urgency.

COUNCILLORS INSPECT FENCE POST

Councillors visited the site of the fence in Victoria Street last Wednesday to view the fence post which had been thrown into the nearby brook.

GIRL PUSHED OVER

A sixteen-year-old girl was pushed over while walking down Milldale Road last Tuesday. There was no apparent motive.

PLANK PROBLEM

Mr Arthur Harmsworth of 10 Ashby Road has eighty-four builders planks in his front garden, a situation which he describes as "crazy".

SCHOOLCHILDREN GO INTERNATIONAL
As a contribution to the festival, schoolchildren staged a concert in the town hall last Tuesday. Organised by Mrs Sandra Bartram, with husband Albert Bartram at the piano, over fifty schoolchildren, dressed in different national costumes, put on a quick-fire programme that featured singing, reciting, ballet and tap-dancing, piano solos and recorder duets interspersed with group dance formations, before a crowded and mainly appreciative audience. A disturbance was caused by a small minority of elderly people in the audience who followed their habit of getting up out of their seats, putting on their coats and leaving before the entertainment had ended.

BAD WEATHER
Councillor Betty Winfield told a meeting of the council on Friday that last week's bad weather was "a matter for regret" and that it had caused her "personal distress". Councillor Frank Bates replied that there was "no point in crying over spilt milk" and that plans for the future were "in hand".

ONLY STEAM
Firemen were called to the public convenience in the market place last Monday, but it turned out to be a false alarm with good intent. The chief fire officer said that it was "only steam".

NO SHORTAGE OF STRING
Two hundred and thirty-four balls of string have been collected during the past month by the Women's Royal Voluntary Service. A spokeswoman said that a decision on what use they were to be put to would be announced shortly.

MORE ATTRACTIVE HALL
Improvements to the Social Hall in the High Street are going ahead. The main window is being blocked up and both the ceiling and floor lowered by six inches, projects which have been mooted many times in the past few years. In

addition a one-way turnstile is to be installed in an attempt to deal with the recurring problem of the elderly people who get up and leave before the end of the entertainment.

SOCIETY ALL SET FOR VIVA MEXICO

The musical society's second production, Viva Mexico, takes to the stage at the Social Hall next week. This light-hearted comedy musical runs from Monday to Saturday. Set in a remote part of the country in the midst of a revolution, Viva Mexico includes such well known songs as 'La Cucaracha', 'Ay-Ay-Ay-Ay' and 'Oh Foolish Moon'. Main character in the show is the son of the owner of the El Rancho Grande, Ramon, otherwise known as the bandit leader El Zorro, played by Graham Crabtree. In an effort to keep production costs to the minimum, members of the society have built the scenery.

In charge of musical direction is Arthur Bramley, who said that the company had high hopes for the show, and were confident that the new turnstile installation would prevent a recurrence of the episode involving the elderly people which had disrupted the first night of last year's production of Fiddler On The Roof.

SOIL TO SPARE

The council has a few tons of soil to spare, councillors heard on Tuesday. Soil from new graves at the cemetery has been used in the past to fill in the nearby brook which has now been piped. Councillor Brecknock told a meeting of the council that no more soil was needed for filling in.

Councillors agreed that the soil should be left at the end of the roadway until it was decided what to do with it.

ANOTHER EVENING'S ENTERTAINMENT SPOILED

A varied evening of choral solos, duets and trios was given by the Townswomen's Guild last week. The shortest and most unexpected item came from Mrs Avis Hickling with her song of a mountain sheep, while Mrs Valerie Scattergood displayed musical versatility with a self-accompanied song to the strain of a mandolin. Before the vote of thanks given by Mrs Bird eight elderly citizens in the audience pulled on their coats and left the hall. Mrs Bird, visibly upset, nevertheless declared the evening a success despite the incident.

RIDICULOUS SITUATION OVER RUBBISH

"Not good enough," was the reaction of members of the Chamber of Trade over the vexed question of the continued non-collection of rubbish from the premises of Mr Arthur Pemberton, greengrocer, of 35 Main Street. In a statement Mr Pemberton said: "Every day I walk across the road and place my sacks of rubbish in the council's refuse vehicle, and every day the council workmen take it out of the vehicle and place it back outside my shop again. They will not explain their actions, I am in the dark."

Councillor Dresser said: "I think this is a ridiculous situation."

SCULPTURE IS SUBJECT

A talk on sculpture was given to members of the Rotary Club on Tuesday. The speaker was Mr Ken Marriott, who told members that he worked entirely on his own in an eight-foot-square studio for sixteen hours a day.

BAND GIVES CONCERT TO UNAPPRECIATIVE AUDIENCE

The Silver Prize Band gave a concert to elder citizens at their club in Broad Street last Thursday. During the evening the conductor announced that the band would perform a medley of tunes, and the audience were invited to guess how many. This invitation was sadly not taken up by members of the audience, who left the hall en masse before the vote of thanks.

THE HOLIDAY COTTAGE

The scene is set in a remote country cottage. It has been raining for four days and nights. The outlook is bleak.

ACT 1

In the kitchen.

HE (*peering through the window*): Rain! Rain! Rain! When is it going to stop?
SHE (*brightly*): Ping-pong?
HE (*curtly*): We burst the ball.
SHE: Cards?
HE: We left them in the pub.
SHE (*drumming her fingers*): Well, what shall we do?
HE (*peering through the window*): We'll think of something.

ACT 2

In the bedroom.

HE is bent face downwards over the bed, naked except for a souwester and wellington boots, his buttocks pushed upwards.

SHE is standing on the other side of the bedroom, dressed only in high-heeled shoes, stockings, suspender-belt and a snorkel mask. She holds a table-tennis bat in her hand.

SHE (*advancing towards him*): Forehand or backhand?

ACT 3

THE FOLLOWING MORNING

In the kitchen.

The kettle is boiling, filling the kitchen with steam.
HE is pacing up and down.
SHE is arranging dried flowers in an egg cup.
The rain still lashes at the windows.

HE (*through gritted teeth*): Here we are in an area noted for its scenic beauty of rugged coastline interspersed with golden beaches and vistas of unsurpassed grandeur, an unspoilt paradise warmed by the caress of the Gulf Stream, of estuaries replete with exotic fish, of meadows filled with unidentified flora, secluded fragrant woods, pre-historic stone circles, ancient fortresses, medieval churches, Elizabethan castles, Napoleonic towers and Georgian mansions, where the forty shades of green stretch as far as the eye can see. And *we* can't even see out of the fucking window! We're stuck here like rabbits in a hutch.

HE squeezes the dishcloth until his knuckles turn white, his eyes shut tight with exasperation.

SHE (*glancing at the kettle*): We need more potatoes.

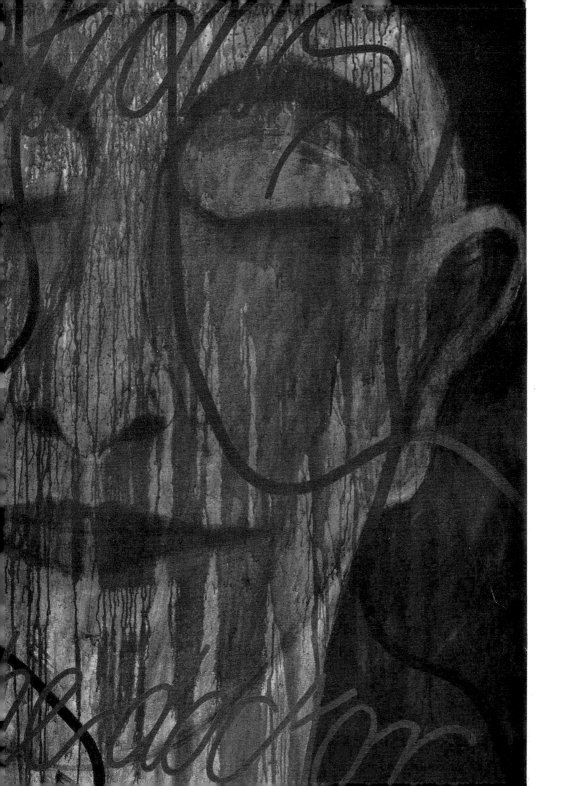

ACT 4

THE NEXT DAY

In the kitchen.

HE (*peering through the window*): The birds are gathering on the wires.
SHE (*looking up from her book*): Poor sods.

THREE HOURS LATER

In the kitchen.

SHE is still reading.
HE is pacing round in circles.
HE (*peering through the window*): The road's flooded. The water's rising.

ACT 5

At the kitchen table.

HE (*dragging his eyes from the table and casting them out the window*): I can't do another jigsaw.

ACT 6

In the bedroom.

The rain beats against the bedroom window.

SHE (*lying in bed stroking the bedpost with thumb and forefinger*): It never lets up.

HE (*a muffled voice beneath the bedclothes*): Now?
SHE (*plunging her finger into the jar of cream*): The big toe. (*pause*)
Mmmmmm. (*running her fingers through the knuckles of the other hand*):
Ooh yes, in between. (*pause*) Now the instep.
HE (*his upturned palm emerging from beneath the bedclothes*): More cream.
SHE (*writhing*): The other one. The other one. (*turning over onto her stomach, her face pressed into the pillow*) Squeeze!
HE: Both together? Tell me when.
SHE: Tighter. (*gripping the iron bars of the bedhead between her teeth, her palms flat against the wall*) Aaaahh!
(*pause*)

He straddles her buttocks, his hands pressed on her shoulderblades. He scratches her back with his fingernails, from the nape of her neck to the base of her spine.

HE: Like this?
SHE: Left shoulderblade.
HE: Enough?
SHE: More! More!
HE: Say when.
SHE: Now the powder. (*pause*) Mmmm. Just like a baby.
HE (*enveloped in a cloud of powder*): Last days of Rome!
SHE (*turning over*): Now the front.
HE (*thrusting his fingers into her ears*): Say when! Say when!
SHE (*excitedly*): Float like a butterfly!
HE (*exultantly*): Sting like a beeeee!

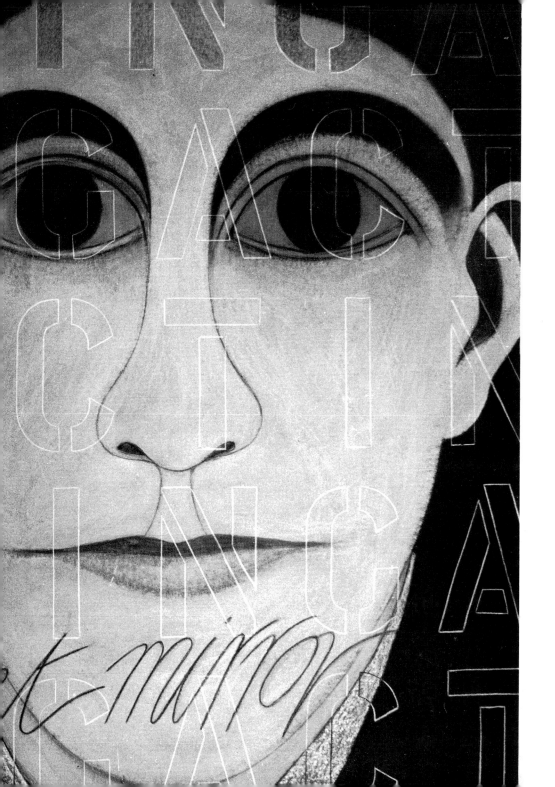

ACT 7

TWO DAYS LATER

It is still raining.
HE and SHE are sitting naked on either side of the kitchen table, applying cream from tubes while counting insect bites.

HE: Twenty-seven.
SHE: Twenty-three.
HE: How many more days?
SHE: Six.

ACT 8

THREE DAYS LATER

In the bedroom.

The rain beats against the window behind the bed, on which HE is lying naked on his back. His arms are stretched out on either side, his wrists tied tightly with nylon stockings to the iron bedposts at the top of the bed. His legs are open, stretched out, each ankle tied to the bedposts at the bottom of the bed. His mouth is gagged with a piece of cloth.
SHE is standing on the far side of the bedroom, smiling. She stubs out her cigarette in the ashtray on the bedside table and climbs onto the bed. She kneels astride, facing him. She unbraids her long hair and trails it across his body and face.
Sweat breaks out on his forehead. as he writhes helplessly. His eyes shut tight. His teeth bite into the gag. His fingernails dig into his palms. Spasms run through him from head to foot. He thrashes from side to side, then slowly subsides.

SHE straightens up and smiles.

His breathing returns to normal. His eyes begin to close.

ONE HOUR LATER

HE awakes.

SHE is no longer in the room.

The rain has stopped.

A breeze stirs the curtains.

The sun shines through the window onto his face.

The sweat has dried on his body. He shivers.

His movements have tightened the knots in the stockings which secure his hands and feet. He flexes his fingers and toes, and shifts position as best he can, to ease the numbness in his limbs.

Outside the window the sky is blue. A seagull sits on the window ledge watching him.

The sun begins to set. The sky through the window is red.

The wind has dropped. HE can hear the sound of the waves breaking against the foot of the cliffs below the cottage, and the raucous calls of the rooks coming home to roost. In the distance the cries of the curlews in the estuary.

The light begins to fade.

A moth settles on his face.

A spider spins a web between the bedpost and the wall.

It becomes dark.

THE MASK

Worn too often the mask begins to remould the features of the face beneath. And as the face grows older so too does the mask until, like an old glove, it wears thin and becomes so threadbare that it is a mere cowl which no longer quite keeps out the cold, the rain, the noise and the harsh light. Sometimes it is loose and slack like a second skin. At other times it is a taut membrane, too broad a smile would split it. So the face beneath, no longer cocooned, no longer grimaces, laughs and shouts, but sets and concentrates, fearful of a sudden sneeze. And should a cool wind brush the forehead or a warm hand caress the cheek then the face freezes lest a tremor might burst the gossamer shroud. Shaded no more against the sun it hides in shadows. But in the shadows the rain drums on the skin stretched tight over the cheekbones and the mask is a flayed hide. Day in day out. The skin of the mask is now so taut over the skin of the face that tears are trapped in the eyes and cannot flow. The lips are drawn back from the teeth and the mouth is fixed in a permanent grin. In the morning the mask in the mirror is a stranger, by evening an old friend.

OUR BOY

Our boy.
The image of his father.
Still in his pram when he gave Mrs Johnson the shock of her life.
As a toddler so hasty that he ate bananas with the skins on.
Such a little joker that he did his business in our Joyce's shoe.
Then carved SORRY on the back of her hairbrush with his penknife.
So thrifty that he saved the pickings from his nose in a matchbox.
The same one that he kept his caterpillars in.
Never threw anything away.
So humane that he always put worms and slugs out of their misery.
So playful that he bounced little Sharon round the room.
Even off the walls.
What a boy!
A young lion.
He could have been a Black Belt.
Never backed down in an argument.
Guaranteed to hold his own.
And generous to a fault.
Bought everybody a drink. Even those who didn't want one.
Always looked after his mother.
Lovely boy.
Full of fun.
He'd travel on the last train home with half a cucumber stuck down his

trousers and a bright red nose.

Or stand outside phone boxes then tap on the glass.

And in bus queues! Dear oh dear!

A real caution.

Wrote out that cheque for a parking ticket on his private parts and said to the secretary behind the desk: "Here you are darling, cash this!"

What a lad!

And so determined.

He swore he'd teach the cat to beg for its dinner or die trying.

And he did, poor boy.

It preyed on his mind.

But he was our boy.

One in a million.

Never be another one like him.

THE OLD MINE

A mile out of the village the road forks to the right and after half a mile reaches the old slate quarry. Fifty years ago the miners quarried the slate for low wages, from dawn until dusk in unsafe conditions. The quarry owners neglected all safety regulations. One day the cracked ledge under which the miners were working collapsed and buried ten miners under a thousand tons of rock.

The quarry has been closed for many years now. Only one of the original miners remains, in a tied cottage on the road alongside the quarry, coughing away his last few years in rooms lit by 40-watt bulbs. His job is to look after the monument to the dead which has been built on top of the slagheap. The quarry is now a council rubbish dump where people from the local villages come to throw their household garbage sacks, which are then torn open and eaten by a colony of gigantic pigs.

But soon dead calves, stinking fish and poisons are dumped in large quantities, so that eventually a man is employed by the council to supervise the rubbish. One evening he and the old miner lean on the five-barred gate, smoking their pipes and gazing down at the pigs eating their way through the garbage in the quarry below. The miner says that there is a particular spot between the pigs' shoulderblades which, if scratched, will cause the beasts, fierce as they are, to roll over onto their backs in harmless bliss. The next day the man in charge of the rubbish decides to give it a try.

A huge sow which is belly-deep in garbage is snorting and grunting as it rips open a black plastic sack. The sow eyes the man warily as he approaches, its

snout deep inside the bag of reeking vegetables. Gingerly he scratches the pig's back in the place so precisely described to him by the miner. But the miner omitted to tell him in which direction to scratch. The sow, rubbed up the wrong way, squeals, turns and sinks its teeth into his leg. Cursing he pulls his leg from the sow's mouth, leaving half his shin between its teeth. He staggers backwards, treading into a heap of rotting potatoes beneath which a gorged boar is sleeping. He steps on the boar which grips him by the ankle between its jaws. He is stuck. The loss of blood from his shin soon weakens him. He slips. The sow now has him by the shoulder. Grunting and squealing the boar and the sow shake him like a disputed bone.

Woken from their slumbers by the noise, thirty other pigs rise out of the garbage and lumber from all directions towards the potato heap. The miner, taking a nap after his dinner, is also woken by the din. He leans out of his cottage window and fires a shotgun blast across the quarry. The pigs scatter. The mutilated man sinks into the mire and is suffocated by the mashed potatoes.

THE BLUE COTTAGE

A local man is hired by the owner of a holiday cottage to do some garden clearance in her absence. He is instructed by letter to remove three unwanted hedges, clear an area of shrubs, chop down two trees and dig up the lawn prior to resowing at a later date. It is the blue cottage on the hill. Between the writing of the instructions and the time he receives the letter (the post being slow in those parts) another holiday cottage on the hill has also been painted blue, and it is there that he carries out the work in the owner's absence; when she arrives for the summer she finds that her garden has been drastically pruned. She becomes distraught. When the owner of the first blue cottage also arrives for the summer and discovers that her garden remains an untended wilderness she accuses the owner of the other blue cottage of stealing her labourer. There is an argument. One woman smacks the other's face, detaching her retina. A lengthy lawsuit follows, then a feud lasting seven years. Though neighbours, they never speak to each other. Eventually the tense, silent summers wear them both down and they sell their cottages. The gardener wins the National Sweepstake and retires to Florida, where his landscaped gardens are tended by a retinue of servants under his careful guidance.

THE BRIDGE

A fisherman is fishing the evening rise in a pool below the five-arched bridge. On the bridge is parked a car in which sit a courting couple holding hands. They have sat in a car each Monday, Wednesday and Saturday evening for the past fifteen years. During those years he has changed his car three times and the bridge has been tarmacadamed twice. They have never married: she is a Catholic, he is a Protestant. Both are now middle-aged. Each night, as they leave, she carefully takes the engagement ring off her finger and puts it back into its velvet-lined box in her handbag.

THE SOCIAL SCENE

BRIGHT IDEA FOR BIN BAGS

The Conservation Society spring meeting heard that dustbin day will be a brighter affair from now on. The District Council is to introduce yellow dustbin bags, instead of black ones, in an attempt to "bring a little colour into Tuesdays," a spokesman said. According to the council's Environment Committee the new, brighter bags do not cost any more, are the same strength, and are easier to see in the dark and in fog.

AN UNUSUAL TALK

The Townswomen's Guild speaker for the March meeting was Miss Renee Cresswell, who gave an unusual talk entitled "The Life Of A Woman Butcher". Miss Cresswell became a butcher during the last war after abandoning her original intention of becoming a professional musician. Her work has ranged from making sausages to slaughtering animals.

The meeting closed with a collection for Mother Teresa's Mission Amongst the Lepers in Calcutta.

CHEESE AND WINE

At a Cheese and Wine Gathering of the Friendship Club last Thursday, the guest speaker was Mr A.K. Wendy, Professor of Morbid Anatomy and Histo-Pathology, who took as his subject "Sudden Death". A somewhat subdued company heard how advances in health, hygiene and immunology had still failed to remove the possibility of sudden and unexpected death striking anyone at any moment.

ETHEREAL MEETING

The monthly meeting of the Ethereal Society opened with a silent exhortation by Mrs Ivy Childs. After a short pause, Mr Cyril Spring gave a demonstration of feather arrangement in a thimble. The evening ended with a finger buffet and a poem.

MODERN MOTHERS

A well attended meeting of the Modern Mothers Coffee Club last Wednesday heard a talk by the Reverend Cyril Thompson entitled "Lighting Up Darkest Africa". The minister said that preaching the Christian gospel in Africa was very different from preaching in England. He recalled how the first time he ascended an African pulpit a string of camels passed by outside the door, and that the congregation consisted entirely of topless African women who caused him "some embarrassment" when they took communion.

After the meeting a collection was taken for Mother Teresa's Mission in Calcutta.

TROMBONIST DIES

The Silver Prize Band's secretary, Arthur Sharp, died while taking part in a band concert at the Community Hall last Thursday. Mr Sharp had just finished "The Bold Gendarmes" in a trio with two other trombone players in the band, Mr Denis Plackett and Mr Lionel Russell. While the audience were applauding he collapsed and was carried backstage, where he was found to be dead.

SNOWY WASTES

At a joint meeting of the Eight O'Clock Club and the Men's Thursday Club at the Methodist Centre, the speaker was Mr P. Beeding. With the use of a film strip, made by himself, he spoke about his recent trip to Antarctica. He said that in the Antarctic the weather conditions were wet and cold, with large icebergs and frequent snow. He urged anyone intending to make the journey to "be prepared".

LINER NURSE

The Townswomen's Guild last Thursday heard how Miss Dorothy Mangold came to be a nurse in charge on a liner with two thousand passengers and eight hundred crew. Besides recounting many amusing anecdotes about the different forms of sickness on board ship, she also described how she helped with entertainments. The Spithead Review was recalled and also her meetings with famous people, including the Queen of Tonga, whose exceptional height presented some difficulties in her cabin.

The meeting ended with a silver collection for Mother Teresa and her helpers which yielded £15.

FILM SHOW

The Cine Society last week saw an evening of films by Mr Harold Gandy. The first was a film about bees, which Mr Gandy had set to music. This was followed by a film about the Isle of Wight, although sound recording problems caused this to be cut, and the last one was a compilation of films showing every Bonfire Night in the town since the war.

DOG GYMKHANA

A dog gymkhana recently held by the District Dog Club was a great success, with more than fifty dogs and an equal number of people taking part. The event was organised by Fiona Carleton and judged by Paddy Heyhoe, who faced an unenviable task.

Winners were: Baron (Best Condition); Shep (Best Veteran); Shandy (Waggiest Tail); Roger (Longest Tail); Jock (Shortest Tail); Eric (Best Trick and Chase Me Charlie); Susie (Dog The Judge Would Most Like To Take Home); Marjie (Button Race); Shane (Obstacle Race); and Oscar (Most Virile).

WORLD-WIDE COOKERY

At the monthly meeting of the Good Companions, Mrs Ditcham spoke about "A Cook's Tour", covering North Norway, the Isle of Wight, Zimbabwe, the German Black Forest and West Point Military Academy. She described the food of each place and how it was prepared. The competition for the prettiest weed was won by Mrs Prentice and the competition for something made on the spur of the moment from a paper serviette was won by Mrs Squires.

FIRST AID DILEMMA

The First Aid League's last competition of the current season set an intriguing problem. Two teenage girls camping out had run into difficulties. One girl had become completely covered from head to toe by a swarm of bees while asleep. Her companion lay beside her in a state of catatonic shock, her fists clenched and her legs tightly crossed. The First Aiders' solution to this unusual accident was described by the adjudicator, Mr Jack Neep, as "a triumph of ingenuity".

MIXED DAY FOR OCTOGENARIANS

The annual day out of the Octogenarians' Club was marred by the death of one of its members, Mr Arnold Digby, shortly after getting onto the coach. By a show of hands it was decided that "the show must go on", and a visit to the gas showrooms was followed by a cold ham tea and an evening's entertainment by the Blind Choir.

MEETING WRECKED

The local branch of the Society For The Preservation of Rural England met last Tuesday to discuss vandalism, but had to abandon their meeting when hooligans bombarded the village hall with bricks, bottles and milk crates. The chairman of the society, Mr Thrush, said "This highlights the problem."

WILDLIFE VISIT

The Evergreen Club's secretary, Mrs F.M. Waller, organised an outing to the Wildlife Park. Members enjoyed a pleasant afternoon and were particularly fascinated by the peacocks who displayed their feathers effectively.

ACCOMPANYING

At the Co-operative Women's Guild April meeting, Miss Enid Beeton explained and demonstrated the art of providing a musical accompaniment, the seven songs of varied moods being sung by Beryl Wheeler.

Practising was all-important said Miss Beeton, but she explained that the height of the piano stool was crucial. Miss Beeton concluded with a demonstration of piano stool positioning.

AFTERNOON INSTITUTE

At the annual meeting of the Afternoon Institute posies were presented to Mrs Parkinson and Mrs Pitt. Mrs Joan Thistle gave a talk and demonstration entitled "Lampshades In A Hurry", and Mrs Bunty Wood related some of her amusing stories about wasps. It was agreed that the proceeds from the bring-and-buy sale should be donated to Mother Teresa's Mission in Calcutta.

HAPPY CIRCLE

The meeting of the Happy Circle opened with hymns and prayers led by the Rev. Hancock. The circle's oldest member, Mrs Doris Finch, celebrated her ninety-first birthday. In the absence of the arranged speaker, due to illness, members played games of bingo.

CAR BOOT SALE

There were eleven open car boots filled with parsnips at the saleground on bank holiday Monday. This unusual method of marketing the local crop was conceived by Mr Noel Thirst. The District Ladies' Lifeboat Guild was in attendance.

FORGET-ME-NOT EVENING

At the birthday meeting of the Forget-Me-Not Club, organised in aid of Mother Teresa's Mission, Mrs Van Poortliet gave a talk entitled "A Kaleidoscope of Buttons", and Mrs Moorby gave a Jam and Jelly demonstration. They were thanked by Mrs Gorme. Several members agreed to form a darts team. The recipe competition was won by Mrs Rita Watson with her "Chicken in a Saucepan".

ADVENTUROUS OUTING

The Adventurers Club, well known locally for their unusual exploits, went to the grass roots of every picnic's central ingredient, the vacuum flask, when they made tea at the Thermos factory last Wednesday as part of National Tea-Making Fortnight. Most of the Thermos workforce was on holiday, but the furnace stayed alight. When production is in top gear it melts the glass for vacuum flasks at a rate of one ton per hour and holds about sixty tons of molten glass at any one time.

Sweltering in the heat from the giant furnace, the twenty-six Adventurers brewed tea throughout the afternoon, and despite some setbacks such as teaspoons being too hot to handle, six members of the club being overcome by the heat, and the butter for the teacakes melting into liquid, the chairman of the Adventurers, Wayne Grimmer, nevertheless declared the day a success.

FLORAL MENU

The Hotel Norman is presenting a special menu for the Floral Week in July. The Floral Meal will consist of nettle and watercress soup, beef steak Tudor Rose, lime sorbet and crystallised violets.

BEAN '84

Five hundred and eight people attended the Runner Bean Society's annual show, held in the supertent on the Common last Saturday.

The winner of the Sponsored Bean Contest was Mr Wilf Bestwick, who was presented with the Bean '84 trophy, a silver replica of a runner bean. Mr Bestwick had grown a bean twenty inches long.

Amongst the many stalls and sideshows an exhibition of bean sculpture by Mr Wilton Render attracted special attention.

All proceeds from the show were donated to the Mother Teresa Mission for Lepers in Calcutta.

PENSIONERS VOICE

The spring meeting of the No. 1 branch of Pensioners Voice was attended by thirteen members. They were welcomed by the chairman and various reports were given. It was decided to send a letter of thanks to Mrs Budgen for cleaning the bus shelter.

Results of the competition for a covered coat hanger were: 1st, Mrs Pettit; 2nd, Mrs Stokoe; 3rd, Miss Tubbs.

The competition for a kitchen utensil hat was won by Mrs Tomes, and the competition for a vegetable person by Mrs Purse.

The guest speaker was Mrs Jones, who spoke on bones.

SPONGE SURPRISE

The Midweek Society's 39th annual spring show took place at the Village College last Wednesday. The biggest surprise of the show was a win in the Victoria Sponge class by sixty-nine-year-old Agnes Gamble, who beat forty-two other competitors, including her mother. The show judge for home produce, Mrs Tring, said that it was "a remarkable sponge".

TOILET PROBLEMS

The annual general meeting of the Men's Institute heard Chairman R.V. Strivens state that once again complaints had been received about the condition of the toilets. Mr Strivens said that this was the fifth successive year that a complaint had been made about the toilets. Mr Green promised to look into it.

EXTRAORDINARY MEETING

An extraordinary emergency meeting of all local social societies was held yesterday in the Community Hall, to discuss the controversial topic of the collection of money, supplies and produce for Mother Teresa's Mission Amongst the Lepers in Calcutta.

Representatives from The Townswomen's Guild, The Conservation Society, The Octogenarians, The Gardening Society, The Friendship Club, The Ethereal Society, The First Aid League, The Modern Mothers' Coffee Club, The Notherners Association, The Cine Society, The Co-operative Women's Guild, The District Dog Club, The Runner Bean Society, The Silver Prize Band, The Eight O'Clock Club and The Men's Thursday Club packed the hall

to hear this extraordinary debate on whether the donations to Mother Teresa were, in the words of the Reverend Cyril Tomlinson, "the least we can do to help those less fortunate than ourselves", or, in the words of Major Carson, "throwing good money down the drain". The meeting heard the chairman, Mr George Fairclough, say that improvisation and making do with very little were the main characteristics of Mother Teresa's Mission. He described how she opened a school for children with just earth for a blackboard and a stick to write on it. And how, in her work among the poor, diseased and dying of Calcutta, she does not wait for favourable conditions but takes the lepers to hospital in a wheelbarrow when no other transport is available.

Mrs Roberts said that Mother Teresa uses five miles of bandage every day for her lepers, and that it was on the purchase of bandages that most of the money collected had been spent.

Mr Molyneux replied that there were rumours that Mother Teresa's lepers used these bandages to make decorative curtains and wall-hangings, and that Mother Teresa herself made her own bandages by tearing up old sheets into strips.

Mrs Childs wondered if the bandages should not be sent to the Sanctuary for Oiled Sea Birds, taking into account the heavy cost of postage to India.

An angry Mrs Plackett said that there was clear evidence that the knitted squares which had been donated for the poor and homeless had all been unpicked by Mother Teresa and her helpers.

An irate Mr Gandy wanted to know why the two thousand rubber bands that had been collected and sent to Calcutta had all been returned.

Reverend Tomlinson said that it was useless to collect rubber bands as Mother Teresa secures her bandages with string.

At this point heckling could be heard from the back of the hall, and after an outburst by Major Carson angry scenes ensued, scuffles broke out, and the meeting was adjourned in uproar.

SAVED FROM THE SURF

Every morning the little old lady takes her Pekinese dog along the promenade and down the steps behind the Oceana Café so that it can shit on the beach. IT IS FORBIDDEN, says the notice at the top of the steps, TO LET DOGS OFF THEIR LEADS UNTIL THEY ARE BELOW THE HIGH WATER MARK. Normally this line of seaweed and driftwood is halfway up the beach, but today is a high spring tide and the surging water reaches almost to the steps, at the foot of which the small dog squats apprehensively on the pebbles soaked with sea spray. Trembling and whimpering it gazes up at its mistress standing on the steps as it strains to force out the turd which protrudes from its dilating arsehole. A big wave crashes onto the dog and drags it back into the surf with hundreds of hissing pebbles. The dog surfaces, whining and barking and paddling frantically with its little legs. Already it is twenty yards from the shore, caught in the undertow. The old lady shrieks for help. A muscular man in a baseball cap and tracksuit who is jogging along the promenade dives in to save the Pekinese. Within seconds he is dragged out to sea, desperately struggling against the grey, heaving swell. With blue light flashing and siren blaring, a Panda car screeches to a halt, two policemen jump out at the double and plunge fully clothed into the pounding waves in a vain effort to reach the drowning man. Impeded by their blue serge uniforms they too are sucked under. The lifeboat is launched and after an hour returns with the three bodies covered with plastic sheets. Eventually the tide turns, washing ashore a baseball cap and two policeman's hats, to one of which is clinging the little dog, soon to be reunited with its tearful and joyous owner. A funeral service is held for the three victims and they are buried in adjacent plots in the graveyard on the hill overlooking the beach.

The extraordinary escape of the gallant little dog was the front page story in the local newspaper. The talk of the town for weeks. Then the weeks became months and years, but the deliverance of the dog from the sea was never forgotten and passed into local legend. And when the old lady eventually breathed her last, to be followed within a week by her pining companion, it was generally felt that some commemorative gesture was called for. So, at the next meeting of the town council it was proposed, and unanimously approved, that a memorial be installed on the promenade at the scene of the dramatic escape, and three months later, on the tenth anniversary of the famous day, the Silver Prize Band played at the top of the steps behind the Oceana Café, and the Lady Mayoress unveiled the plate glass case in a sturdy iron frame to the front of which was affixed the commemorative plaque. In the glass case were the baseball cap, the two policeman's hats, and the Pekinese, a skilfully realised example of the local taxidermist's craft. Beneath the glass case was an iron box with a slot in it for donations to the National Dog Sanctuary.

The memorial case was listed on the town map and during the summer season became a tourist attraction ranking with the floral gardens and the miniature railway. Until, one bank holiday Monday, the sleepy seaside town was invaded by hundreds of leather-clad youths on motor cycles and an equal number of pale-faced boys on scooters. Inflamed by alcohol and pills, their tempers became frayed and a pitched battle was fought on the promenade. Boulders from the beach were thrown by rival gangs, the glass case was shattered and the collection box looted. The baseball cap, the policeman's hats and the stuffed dog were thrown into the sea.

In the aftermath of the violence the prevailing mood in the town was a mixture of anger at the sacrilegious vandalism and sorrow at the loss of the memorial relics. A cloud of sadness hung over the sunny resort. Everyone agreed that the summer was spoilt.

Then came the day of the Sea Angling Contest. Fishermen in quilted anoraks and oilskins lined the beach at twenty-yard intervals. At the foot of the steps behind the Oceana Café competitor number 29 hammered a rod rest into the shingle, baited his hook with a lugworm, then cast the heavily weighted line far out into the surf. Leaning his rod on the rod-rest with the tip pointing towards the sky he poured some soup from his thermos flask, holding the cup in both hands as he hunched his shoulders against the cutting east wind. Conditions could hardly have been worse and as the hours passed he became resigned to a blank day. Down the line the news was passed whenever someone caught a fish, however small. A few dabs, half a dozen little pollock, a tiny bass; but most competitors had, like him, caught nothing. Then, fifteen minutes from the end of the contest, the rod tip curved slowly down towards the waves. Picking up the rod and striking hard over his right shoulder he felt a dull, dragging weight at the end of the line. "Seaweed," he thought, tightening the ratchet as he carefully reeled in and brought the dead weight to the surface. It was the stuffed Pekinese, hooked through the back leg and waterlogged but otherwise well preserved. As the news spread other competitors left their marks and gathered round. The press photographer who was on hand to record the contest took photographs of the angler with the dog cradled in his arms and these were featured in the local newspaper the following week.

Once the dog had been dried out and restored by the taxidermist, the town council soon decided to commission a new memorial case to replace the one that had been so wantonly destroyed. Though hesitating to use the word "miraculous" the vicar in his Sunday sermon made mention of the dramatic deliverance twice over of the dog from the sea and declared it to be remarkable at the very least, a triumph against seemingly insurmountable odds which could serve as a parable for when we feel we are certain to be overwhelmed and stand on the brink of despair. The priest expanded on this theme when he blessed the memorial case after it was unveiled by the Lord Mayor in a simple and moving ceremony behind the Oceana Café. Few eyes were dry amongst the townsfolk who lined the promenade, and yet the tears were not of sadness but of joy, of quiet pleasure and pride that a wrong had been righted, the mascot of the town returned, and now was there for all to see as it stood alone and four-square in the glass case, its little head held high and staring defiantly out to sea. Beneath it was an engraved plaque which read: DELIVERED TWICE FROM THE CRUEL SEA. THANKS BE TO GOD.

THE BUTCHER

The butcher's arms,
sleeves rolled back.
Hands like hams
thumping the slab.
The butcher's ears sprouting hairs.
Knuckle bone brow.
Little
piggy
eyes.
"Meat makes the meal,"
the butcher says, honing the cleaver.
"So, don't mess with the meat or I'll cut your fuckin' hands off."

TREVOR'S NIGHT OUT

Trevor was a train spotter. Only at weekends though. From Monday to Friday he sat at his desk and did his job. Keeping the books. He was the quiet one in the office. The girls from the typing pool used to say: "He's a quiet one that Trevor." They'd wink at him as they walked past. Trevor would blush to the roots of his ginger hair. And when the lads in the back room were telling jokes he would cough nervously and begin to sharpen the pencils on his desk, his ears burning. Church mice were fierce and bold compared to Trevor.

Then came the night of the office party. The whip was three hundred pounds and Trevor had paid his share, dutifully week after week, too timid to refuse. He'd hoped to slip away unnoticed. But the lads all said: "Raight then Trevor, yer've paid yer wack, nah cum on aht from beyond that there desk an lets be ayin yer. Sup up yoth!" And they slapped him on the back while the girls from the typing pool giggled and sniggered as Trevor smiled weakly and said, " Just a half for me please."

"Just a half! Eyup, hark at that! Just a bloody half! Bogger me! Ere yer daft wassock, get that dahn yer!"

There was no getting out of it. From the office to the pub, from the pub to the club. "GerranutherpintinferTrevor! Un mek it snappy soree!"

Until the whip ran out, so the lads from the back room and the girls from the typing pool all went off singing at the top of their voices to the disco and Trevor hurried off unsteadily to catch the last bus home.

The bus crept through the suburbs, stopping at every stop. Trevor sat on the top deck, his bladder bursting. He crossed his legs and bit his lip. Hot flushes and cold sweats soaked him through to his vest until, three stops away from home, he could hold out no longer. He scurried down the stairs, jumped off the slowly moving bus and ran full pelt down the alley by the side of the supermarket. It was pitch black but his eyes were screwed up tight as he staggered the last few yards, fumbling with the zip on his trousers, and gasped with sheer relief as he emptied his bladder through the wire mesh fence. Then out of the darkness a huge Alsatian guard dog hurled itself against the other side of the fence, barking and snarling, its teeth pressed against the wire as Trevor stood helplessly pissing into its slavering jaws.

Trevor was struck dumb with fright. He never spoke again. Not that he really needed a voice for the train spotting, nor even for the book-keeping, and by the practised use of self-effacing shrugs and gestures he cleverly concealed his dumbness so that no one noticed. And every now and then one of the girls from the typing pool would smile and say, "He's a real quiet one that Trevor."